A GOLDEN HAND WARRIOR

A GOLDEN HAND WARRIOR

AN IMMORTAL CURSE

MONIKA SINGH

PARTRIDGE

A Penguin Random House Company

To order additional copies of this book, contact
Partridge India
000 800 10062 62
www.partridgepublishing.com/india
orders.india@partridgepublishing.com

CONTENTS

DEDICATED TO:

MY MOTHER, MRS. ANITA SINGH;MY FATHER MR. BHUPENDRA SINGH, MY BROTHERS, ABHISHEK SINGH AND VIVEK SINGH, MY BEST FRIEND, SHREYASH GOVIND GUPTA; AND LAST BUT NOT THE LEAST, AKASH SINGH AND ADITI SINGH

ACKNOWLEDGEMENTS

No one can do anything alone. From the person who writes and to the person who publishes, everyone has an important role.

So, I would like to thank-

1. GOD, for his blessings.

2. Mr. Shreyash GovindGupta, who did put his heart and soul to edit my book and always helped me in my ups and downs. He gave me an inspiration to write this book. Though, he had his examinations, but he never declined to read my book and to give reviews upon it. He showed immense support, motivation and always encouraged me to complete this book. So, he has an important role in my life and I want to thank him from the core of my heart. Since, due to him this book is completed

3. My readers.

4. My teachers, Mr. Shailesh Shukla, Mrs. Soniya Mukhergi and Ram Rakhcha

5. My family, who always showed their support and love towards me.

6. My school friends, Sudeshna Singh, Avichal Baranwal, Shruti Choudhary, Saurabh Dubey and Saif khan. MY ILLUSTRATER MR. AADESH who has given beautiful pictures and the amazing cover page. Special thanks to my brother ABHISHEK SINGH who supported me all the time and took care of the every work regarding the book.

7. Off course, my publishers who showed their immense faith on me AND everyone who was involved with me during writing this.

ANALASKA

ANALASKA, a kingdom created by lord of heaven ARMMANDO and lord of hell HEAZER. This kingdom is ruled by its king name LORD NELISH and his wife JUBEELIA. ANALASKA was a very different kingdom, it was quite impossible to know all the deep secrets, which was hidden in the heart of this huge kingdom. Even the king of this kingdom, LORD NELISH was unaware about all the astonishing facts of this kingdom. LORD NELISH have a brother name JUDASE who was very strange from all the people, neither he used to speak a lot nor he did try to be friendly with anyone, not even with his own brother LORD NELISH.

LORD NELISH was a very calm and composed king; he always gave priorities to the matter of his kingdom because he promised his father that he will take care of his kingdom, entirely. LORD NELISH lost his parents, LORD CEREAL AND QUEEN ELIZABETH in a very mysterious mishap. From then onwards NELISH used to consider himself a hapless son for his parents. No one in the kingdom was able to explore the secrets behind the death of their lord and queen but as the years passed, everyone accepted LORD NELISH as the king of the kingdom. ANALASKA had friendly relations with a kingdom named "DION'S kingdom" which was ruled by LORD DION. JUBEELIA was the daughter of lord DION. When LORD NELISH was 17 years old, he visited DION'S kingdom for the first time with the reason of some kingdom related matters. While going to the DION's kingdom he saw a beautiful girl riding on black horse. From the first glance of her smiling face, LORD NELISH found his heart fallen in love. He was not able to forget her face, her smile and the happiness of the air blowing around. When he reached to the LORD DION's kingdom, DION introduced his daughter JUBEELIA, seeing her again LORD NELISH got convinced with the feelings of his heart, that he is truly fallen in love with her. The same condition was there with JUBEELIA, after the first meet with LORD NELISH, she was fallen in her deep thoughts, she used to murmur alone in her room, laugh without any reason and even she lost her sleep. In the nights she used to secretly watch LORD NELISH and used to admire him and think of him. LORD NELISH was in love and always admired JUBEELIA while talking to her but then also he never gained get the courage to tell her about his feelings. A night came, when in dreams LORD NELISH saw his parents but suddenly he woke up and saw JUBEELIA staring at him. He stood up and asked JUBEELIA to stay away from him, then and there he decided to go back to ANALASKA. NEXT MORNING he left DION'S kingdom without even meeting JUBEELIA. JUBEELIA didn't understand the reason behind such behavior of NELISH but still her heart truly not allowed her to forget about him and this condition was noticed by lord DION. He asked JUBEELIA about her hidden feelings and she revealed everything. Lord DION became very happy instead of getting angry, he understood his daughter's feelings and emotions and even agreed for her relations with LORD NELISH. After returning from DION'S kingdom lord

NELISH was not well, he was not able to convince his heart, his dreams were also not supporting him. Lastly, NELISH told everything to ALBERT CRUZ his very good friend and the minister of ANALASKA, after listening everything . . . . ABLERT said, "My lord you are deeply fallen in love with JUBEELIA and you can't escape from this truth, you need to accept this. Don't punish her and stop blaming yourself for your parents' mishap." Getting agreed with ALBERT's thought NELISH decided to propose JUBEELIA and sent a letter to her which told each and every feeling blowing in his heart. Being very happy JUBEELIA told everything to her father and he became ready for their marriage. JUBEELIA decided to worship LORD ARMMANDO for the gift he has given to her. After so many days LORD ARMMANDO became very happy seeing the devotion of her for him and he came in front of her. Seeing ARMMANDO in front . . . . , JUBEELIA stopped while chattering the mantras and then LORD ARMMANDO said, "my daughter, I am very glad seeing your devotion and I am here to bless you, I am going to give you a super natural power that you can use only for once in your life; you will have a time in your life when you will have to choose between evil and pious and the choice which you will make that would decide the future of ANALASKA either bright or in dark. JUBEELIA thought ARMMANDO thinks that she is very stupid and she said, "My lord you think I am so stupid that I can't differentiate between good and bad?" Lord ARMMANDO smiled and said," my child if I have thought so then tell why would I am giving you such great responsibility . . . . Don't worry!!! The time will tell you everything because you are the only one who has the power and the courage to give birth to a great warrior. After saying these words lord ARMMANDO disappeared and left JUBEELIA in a huge dilemma. JUBEELIA tried to find the answers behind the blessings but she was unsuccessful. The day came when JUBEELIA AND NELISH got married and she begun with her new life. She made two very close friends VAROCIA wife of CAPRION the LORD OF ARMY and AEYRENA wife of ALBERT CRUZ. The mob of the kingdom were very happy after getting its queen, from then lord NELISH overcame his hapless thoughts from his mind and heart and began to live a new life with his lady love. In between all such kinds of happiness, something wrong was going on under the eyes of the king but he was not able to see it at all. Every night when the whole ANALASKA fallen in sleep JUDASE, younger brother of LORD NELISH .... goes to somewhere and hides himself so that no one can see him. What he does or where he goes no one was aware about it .... but one day came, when a solider saw him at night going to PIERO the graveyard of the prisoners of ANALASKA, the solider name CLAOSE followed him and saw that JUDASE was begetting the souls of evils and the dead bodies of the prisoners out of the graves. CLAOSE got afraid and unfortunately one of the evil ghost saw him, he started running from their but then also the ghosts caught him took him to JUDASE. CLAOSE said in anger, "I thought you are just like our king, who thinks of the wellness of the kingdom but I was wrong, actually everyone was wrong about you and I am not going to leave you like this, I will show your real face to everyone". JUDASE laughed on the statement of CLAOSE and said, "no one in this kingdom can do anything of me because no one has the courage and no one has any idea about my powers. You are the most loyal solider of the kingdom .... So today I am going to buy your loyalty through my black powers". Accordingly, JUDASE performed his rituals and owned CLAOSE body, now CLAOSE was dead and one of the evil spirits took over his body. All the souls of the courageous patriots solider, the kings and the queens did not use to go in heaven or in hell, but to the secret room of the palace which was located under the palace but somewhere in middle. These were the savior souls which saved ANALASKA from all kind of evil powers .... that's why JUDASE thought another method to spread evil in the whole kingdom. JUDASE was doing something very mysterious which was hidden from everyone. Days passed away then years, after 5 years of marriage one day JUBEELIA got the beautiful news that she is pregnant. LORD NELISH and the whole ANALASKA got flowed up in the river of happiness, the mob celebrated that day and JUBEELIA sent this news to her father. LORD NELISH announced that when the future of ANALASKA will take birth the WHOLE ANALASKA will have grand party. JUBEELIA was very excited but nervous too and then only, she got the information that her one of the best friend, VAROCIA is also pregnant. JUBEELIA called VAROCIA to the palace to, they both were very happy regarding their pregnancy but VAROCIA was more excited than JUBEELIA because it was the second time VAROCIA was pregnant, she was so unlucky that she gave birth to a dead baby during her first pregnancy and this time she was taking care of herself in a more better way and was not taking any risks, even CAPRION was also taking more care of VAROCIA. During this period, no news came from DION'S kingdom which made JUBEELIA slightly unhappy. Suddenly one day a servant told that JUDASE is sick, he doesn't want to meet anyone and also he doesn't want anyone to visit him to see him. When he would feel well, he himself will come out. After few days he got well and came out and said that he is totally fine now. Eight months passed away but no information of DION'S kingdom came to JUBEELIA; being fed up from all these things lastly she called up CAPRION to the palace and ordered him to go to her father's kingdom and find out why her father is not responding. CAPRION went to DION'S kingdom. When he reached over there he found the situation around the kingdom was something strange but what was it, he didn't understand. He went to the palace to DION, he saw that the kingdom was being ruled by the minister CASCA and LORD DION was not present over there. CASCA handed a letter to CAPRION and said, "what is happening and what will be happening in future, I really don't have any idea about that.... but I want to say that something very bad& unfortunate thing is going happen. Tell the queen the future is in her hand." CAPRION found CASCA saying these words from the core of his heart. That day only CAPRION left and returned to ANALASKA; in the next morning he handed over the letter to JUBEELIA and conveyed all the words of CASCA to her. When JUBEELIA opened that envelope, she found a letter which was written by her own father. In that letter LORD DION wrote his feelings.

MY LOVING DAUGHTER,

I AM VERY HAPPY FOR YOU, AND I AM PROUD OF YOU THAT YOU WILL BE GIVING BIRTH TO THE FUTURE OF ANALASKA. MY BEAUTIFUL JUBEELIA HOW THE TIME PAST AWAY WITHOUT YOU, I REALLY DON'T KNOW BUT I KNOW YOU MUST BE VERY EXCITED AND TENSED TOO AND YOU MUST BE MISSING YOUR MOTHER'S COMPANY ....

BUT UNFORTUNATELY SHE IS NOT WITH US, AND THEN ALSO I KNOW SHE IS AROUND YOU, TAKING CARE OF YOU AND KEEPING HER EYES ON YOUR EVERY ACTION EVEN OF YOUR BABY TOO. I DON'T KNOW HOW TO SAY THIS BUT I AM TIRED NOW, I HAVE LIVED MY LIFE WITHOUT MY LOVE FOR MANY YEARS AND NOW THIS IS THE TIME WHEN I CAN GO NEAR TO MY LOVE.

KINDLY FORGIVE ME FOR BREAKING THE CHAINS OF REAPONSBILITY OF A FATHER AND ME HOPE THAT MY MOB WILL FORGIVE ME TOO. DON'T TRY TO FIND ME, I AM FINE AND I WILL BE FINE. I KNOW THAT YOU WILL BE A GREAT MOTHER FOR YOUR CHILDREN. TAKE CARE OF YOURSELF AND YOUR RESPONSBILTIES.... DON'T TRY TO BE A COWARD LIKE ME. I HAVE GIVEN THE RESPONESBILTY OF THE KINGDOM TO CASCA; HE WILL TAKE CARE OF THE KINGDOM. DON'T WORRY I WILL REACH TO YOUR MOTHER VERY SOON.

YOUR'S LOVING FATHER
LORD DION

After reading the letter JUBEELIA was not able to stop her from crying, tears and tears and tears; she was not able to express her feelings to anyone. However LORD NELISH came to know about this sorrowful news and he went to JUBEELIA'S room. On that day something was wrong, the weather was saying something . . . . it felt as if today is the scariest day of ANALASKA. It was raining very heavily, the thunders were shouting, the sky was changing its color again and again apparently. When NELISH reached to his room he found JUBEELIA shouting in pain, he understood everything and called his all the servants. The women's closed the doors and supported JUBEELIA to bear the pain and to give birth. CAPRION was present in the palace, he saw his servants coming towards him telling that," VAROCIA is going to give birth to a baby today only. You have to come with me now. Please come with me before it's late, her condition is very critical." LORD NELISH listened everything and allowed him to go. Both the women's were now going to turn in mothers; graveyard like silence spread in the ANALASKA, people were able to listen the shouting of two women clearly. It felt as if the nature of ANALASKA was ready to welcome someone very special but why the thunders were getting angry, no one understood. The voices stopped and cry of babies was listened by everyone. The nurses came out of the room and told NELISH," congratulation my lord you have got two baby boys, expressing the happiness LORD NELISH gave his rings to the nurses and asked," everything is fine, JUBEELIA is ok." The nurse replied," yes my lord the queen is totally fine. At the time of birth of the babies, a baby cry came from CAPRION's house; VAROCIA gave birth to a girl. She was also fine and was being extremely happy after seeing her daughter. CAPRION was so happy that he was not able to explain but suddenly the whole happiness changed into a shock when he saw the left hands of his daughter, he noticed that her nerves of left hand was golden in color and the rest of the body was mere like other babies, in comparison to other babies what was different in her, CAPRION AND VAROCIA both of them were unable to understand. They thought that must be god ARMMANDO is so happy on them, that he has sent her a daughter on behalf of him as the savior of the kingdom. In addition to this, something like these conditions was there in the palace too, with regard to both the baby boys' one boy's left hand nerves were in golden and the rest of the body was like other children. No one in the kingdom was able to make a right prediction on this point of the baby. Then ALBERT CRUZ came near to the king and said this boy will truly change the destiny of the kingdom that is why he is different from others and because he is not a mere a child but a savior. The predictions about both of the children were very accurate with regard to the future; the future of ANALASKA was totally going to change and so as the destinies of these children too.

THE MAGI TOOK BIRTH

After the three children as it was announced by the king ANALASKA, everyone was invited in a grand organized party in the palace. CAPRION AND VAROCIA also came to the party to wish the king and queen; VAROCIA went near to JUBEELIA to see the babies and also to show her daughter. When VAROCIA and JUBEELIA met, they hugged and wished each other. When JUBEELIA saw VAROCIA'S DAUGHTER, she was stunned and said," her left hand nerves are golden in color same as my son." VAROCIA looked on the hand of the son of JUBEELIA and noticed that his left hand nerves were also golden in color. They both smiled at each other and thought something by their own virtue. While the party was going on the oldest priest of ANALASKA, SIR KEREYON visited the palace in order to bless both the children. LORD NELISH welcomed him and showed his hospitality. JUBEELIA took both the babies near to KEREYON and put both of them in his lap. SIR KEREYON saw something very astonishing which he was not able to reveal; he gave both the babies back to JUBEELIA and stared at her and said," from the first glance of these children I am in dilemma whether I should tell you amongst all of them are not? I think I will not be able to do so, though you are thinking slightly right but at wrong path; the beginning of the end has begun, be careful while taking the decision JUBEELIA now the time has come. Just try to remember the words of ARMMANDO, THE TIME HAS COME. JUBEELIA: I know what are you trying to say but still I don't understand what I have to do". KEREYON smiled and said," I know dear you are innocent, don't worry the time will teach you everything". After saying these words KEREYON left the palace and moved outside, listening such things about the babies the party became fiasco. In accordance with the children why KEREYON said such things, NELISH murmur to himself. JUBEELIA also left the party and went to her room,

VAROCIA AND AEYRENA both followed her. JUBEELIA entered in her room and started crying heavily. Then VAROCIA tried to convince her," JUBEELIA don't take reference of KEREYON, he must be having confusion he can't be right always. Actually no one can be; how one can say anything about the future of anyone, our destiny is already written . . . . in fact, it's written by someone who is not here so don't upset yourself and just enjoy yourself." JUBEELIA tried to cheer herself and came back to the party. After the party got over, JUBEELIA went to the room of her children, she was not able to understand about the decision which she has to make in future; she was just playing with her bubble thoughts and then LORD NELISH came to the room and said," my love I know you are sad and hiding your feelings &tears please forget everything it might be that KEREYON is confused otherwise why he would say such words for the future of ANALASKA. Just try to forget everything and let's move to our room". They both proceeded for their room. When both of them went out of the room JUDASE entered in the room, he stares both the babies and take the baby in his lap whose hand is normal like humans; he started shouting and said," thank you my lord HEAZER thank you very much you sent someone who is going to spread the evil kingdom, who will own all the powers of an evil, who himself is a pure evil. Yours, this cursing boy ARMMANDO will not be able to do anything". All these words of JUDASE was listened by LUCAS the son of ALBERT CRUZ and he didn't respond on that because he was unaware about all these things. LUCAS was a very different boy of his parents, he neither used to play nor does he speak much. Sometimes his parents used to get in trouble in thinking about him that what he is going to do with his life. Every day LUCAS used to go to the fascinating jungles of ANALASKA and collect pebbles and stones from their; after coming back to home he used to work till the midnight on those pebbles and stones. No one knew why he used to do so and when AEYRENA visited his room, she found that those pebbles and stones have turned into a mirror, she gets a huge shock. One day AEYRENA and ALBERT both took LUCAS to the house of IRISH, oldest foreteller of the kingdom . . . . in order to know the future of their son. They reached the house of IRISH which was quite far from their kingdom and was in the jungle. After reaching, they met IRISH who was making tea; he asked them to sit and said,"

Dear ALBERT can you tell me how this tea is going to be in its taste?" ALBERT said," How it's possible to tell the taste sir before it is made". Again IRISH said," if it's not possible to tell the taste of a tea before it is made then why you came over here for knowing the future of LUCAS before time". ALBERT CRUZ and AEYRENA both of them felt ashamed on themselves and said," sir you know it well that I am in worry because of LUCAS strange behavior, I don't understand what he will do and how he will understand his responsibilities". IRISH laughed loudly on his words and said," my dear when you can't tell the taste of this non-living tea, then how can you predict anything about the future journey of your own living child. I respect your feelings and I can tell you one thing". ALBERT asked," what sir?" IRISH looked in the eyes of LUCAS and said," you will play your role and will help someone who will be having the responsibility of this kingdom, his journey is very crucial because his paths of life has blending with the path of a magi". After saying these words IRISH got three cups of tea and offered it to them. Keeping faith on IRISH, ALBERT and AEYRENA tried to take less tension regarding their son. On other hand, JUBEELIA playing with her children thinking about their names. At that time VAROCIA entered in the room of the queen. Having glance on the face of VAROCIA,

JUBEELIA asked, "Did you think of any name for your daughter?

VAROCIA: "Yes I think MORENA would be best suited on her. And did you think of any name for your babies?"

JUBEELIA: "YES, I too have thought. I think AAZARO and LAVINZO."

VAROCIA: "beautiful names. JUBEELIA I want to say something."

JUBEELIA: "yes say."

VAROCIA: "Actually I am very much worried about our children, I don't think it's too easy to understand but I think the lives of our children are going to be very difficult."

JUBEELIA smiled on her such words and said, "My dear VAROCIA I don't know whether dark or bright our tomorrow would be but always thinking about tomorrow, destroys our today and I don't want this and even I want that you should also stop thinking like this too".

VAROCIA understood her words and became happy and they both started playing with their babies again. Seeing both of them in happy mood, both the fathers also felt happy. Such happiness was symbolizing something but only one person was able to understand this indications and that was JUDASE who himself was going to be responsible for everything. JUBEELIA was not able to come out of her thoughts; she was again and again remembering the words of ARMMANDO and KEREYON. She was not able to come out of the well of her thoughts. Seeing her in such ponder LORD NELISH asked her," JUBEELIA now what is the problem why don't you come out of your thoughts, don't think too much just take care of yourself and our babies". JUBEELIA said," my lord I am not worrying but I am also not able to get out of my thoughts, I think we need to find the solution". LORD NELISH pondered over her this statement and said," I think now the time has come to go to the secret room of the book in order to find the truth". The next morning LORD NELISH, JUBEELIA AND ALBERT CRUZ went to the secret room which was there in midst of the palace. They all entered in the room, LORD NELISH opened the great mysterious book by the specific key and turned the pages. Eventually, the blank book wrote something by itself

κανείςδεν μπορεί να ξεφύγει από το πεπρωμένοτου, αν κάποιος αναμένειμε χαρά ή λύπη γίνεται. πεπρωμένοείναι το πεπρωμένοδεν μπορεί να είναι ήπια, όπωςτογάλα.

ALBERT CRUZ spell those words because he only knew this language, no one else in the kingdom was even aware about this language. After ALBERT spelled those words . . . . the wall behind the book turned into two faces; one face said "let LAVINZO WORSHIP ARMMANDO ONLY DON'T LET HIM GO NEAR THE WORSHIPER OF HEAZER" other face said "DON'T TRY TO RUN FROM YOUR DESTINY, LAVINZO WILL BRING A DRASTIC CHANGE IN THIS KINGDOM, HE WILL BE THE LORD OF EVILS THE GREATEST WORSHIPER OF HEAZER". Listening such terrible things JUBEELIA got afraid and only followed the words of the first wall. From then she became very careful towards LAVINZO and tried a lot to save her son from worshipers of GOD HEAZER, but she did not know that destiny is destiny and JUDASE has started his work. He kept on teaching LAVINZO about his god, his work and his fate. JUBEELIA being very truthful towards her work . . . . never stopped LAVINZO for playing and talking with JUDASE because she doesn't have the smell of JUDASE dream. The days and years passed away LAVINZO, AAZARO AND MORENA became 12 years old. Every night MORENA used to wake up from her dreams and starts whooping, mainly she used to see some kind of unclear visions, from her birth till her this age, the nightmares were following her; she never told anyone about her these visions. She thought that it must be some kind of bad dreams but she was not able to understand that her these nightmares wants to say something; they are continuously coming because they are symbol of something. Every early morning MORENA and her very close friend LORIYA used to go to the jungle to feel the freshness and to practice the bows and arrows. One day AAZARO and LAVINZO also decided to visit the beautiful jungles for hunting. Next morning MORENA AND LORIYA both of them went to the jungle and from other side AAZARO, LAVINZO AND KYREO a very good friend of them also visited the jungle at the same time. After reaching in jungle MORENA started her practice with LORIYA. Suddenly she heard the groaning of animal, she moved towards the sound, when she reached there she found a baby deer, wounded badly, she tore a piece of cloth from her dress and tied it on his hand. The baby deer was still grieving in pain and seeing him like this . . . . MORENA got extremely angry; unfortunately AAZARO reached there to his hunted animal and found MORENA sitting with the animal. The first glance of her beautiful face stroked the heart of AAZARO, he wanted to say something but he became speechless seeing her beauty and kind heart. Evidently, MORENA was quite angry and in her anger she shouted over AAZARO," what do you think of yourself sir? Are you god?,

AAZARO: "No madam!!!"

MORENA: "Then how dare you are, how you can be so cruel and brutal for one's life. Who gave you the right to kill or to take someone's life? Even the god also doesn't forgive the murderers, try to respect the importance of life of others even if they are animals, they do feel the pain and they do get hurt".

After scolding AAZARO so badly MORENA returned to her home with LORIYA. Just like AAZARO, MORENA also got slightly attracted towards him. Not knowing why but she was not able to stop her heart thinking about him and AAZARO was still there in jungle. He was also facing the same condition, he never saw a courageous girl like her. After she left, he felt that he has already met her but not having any idea . . . . where? He was not at all aquatinted with the thought that she is the only girl who will change his life. At home MORENA was fighting with her heart's feelings and kept on murmuring about AAZARO," what the hell he thinks of himself, how dare he is and how desperate; didn't you see LORIYA, I have never seen such brutal and cruel boy like him".

LORIYA: "why don't you take his thoughts out of you, everything is fine now just don't bother much and that deer is also fine; we will go tomorrow again to the jungle to see it ok".

MORENA looked LORIYA and said, "Why are you taking his side, do you like him or what? . . . . No, actually I think he must be your friend or future husband but he is my enemy from now".

LORIYA: "you are saying that he is my something but only you are speaking continuously about him, hardly matters bad words; ok fine now let's finish it and try to cheer up your mood".

From behind the curtain VAROCIA was listening everything, she came in front of MORENA and said," my kind hearted daughter, as you can't read anyone's mind . . . . so; you can't blame anyone for their mistakes. May be he was practicing like you and by miss chance he injured the deer". MORENA got herself cold and started thinking of her words whatever she said in her reprisal mood. Apparently something like this was also going on with AAZARO, he was standing near his room window and thinking MORENA, her face, her words, her kindness and mainly her anger won AAZARO'S heart; it seems as if a young boy AAZARO has fallen in love with a girl, who scolded him very badly that no one did with him, yet. That night MORENA was watching those visions again and this time she saw a boy looking same as AAZARO and suddenly she woke up from her dream and started thinking about him. She talked to herself," how can this happen to me, why that boy is coming in my dream, how it's possible". She got up from her bed, came near to the window and started staring the sky. Her heart was fighting with her mind and MORENA was becoming a victim of heart, without knowing anything about that boy her heart made him special for her. Next morning VAROCIA visited the palace in order to meet JUBEELIA. JUBEELIA was pondering and VAROCIA broke her concentration by saying," hello our highness, can I meet you?

JUBEELIA: "off course! My best friend, how are you doing?"

VAROCIA: "I am doing well but I think you are doing the same."

JUBEELIA: "no nothing is like that I was just thinking about AAZARO."

VAROCIA: "what! Is everything all right?"

JUBEELIA: "yes everything is fine but AAZARO is behaving different, he don't eat much, he talks very less and even he is not coming much out of his room. VAROCIA: "so why you are worrying so much just go and talk to him that what is the problem.",

JUBEELIA with helpless eyes: "I went to his room to talk to him but he is not ready to tell me anything." . . . .

VAROCIA smiled and said: "ok!!!!Fine!!! Now I will go and talk to him and I am sure he will surely tell me everything."

VAROCIA goes to the room of AAZARO. VAROCIA enters in the room of AAZARO and he is standing near the window and looking the whole ANALASKA.

VAROCIA: "having a look over the kingdom? Our new king!"

AAZARO turns towards VAROCIA and chuckles: "no just seeing its beauty and peace."

VAROCIA smiles and says: "then why your heart is not in peace?"

AAZARO get stunned and says: "who told you that my heart is not peace?"

VAROCIA: "whoever said this is not important but how these things are happening with you is important and why, what is the reason behind this sudden change."

AAZARO: "I don't know why I am behaving like that but something has changed in me."

VAROCIA with her brows up says: "what?"

AAAZRAO: "I guess my feelings for someone and I even don't know anything about her."

VAROCIA chuckles and says: "Oh My god! AAZARO I think you have fallen in love with that girl about whom you are talking now."

AAZARO: "really, do you think so but still I don't have any idea about that girl, I even don't know her name!!!!"

VAROCIA shows her sympathy to AAZARO by moving her hands on his head and says," if you really love her than till your youth you will remember her and never let your these thoughts go out of you, just keep her image in your heart and focus on your work; if this is true love than I am very sure you will meet her again. AAZARO kisses hand of VAROCIA and say," I hope your words will be true". VAROCIA leaves his room and get back to JUBEELIA and tells everything to her, she also convinced her to respect his feelings. When VAROCIA came back to her home she found MORENA practicing with the swords with CAPRION, VAROCIA found MORENA being dominant over CAPRION; she was extremely good and VAROCIA felt as if MORENA is a warrior and her way of fighting is like, she is much trained in such studies.

VAROCIA: "ok now! Stop it both of you, dear daughter you go to the market and get some spices please."

MORENA: "sure mother!!!!"

As MORENA leaves, VAROCIA talks to CAPRION.

VAROCIA: "my lord I want you to teach the techniques related to war to MORENA."

CAPRION: "I was thinking the same, she is quite good."

VAROCIA: "I don't think she is only good but her attitude and her way of fighting is the indicator of a warrior."

CAPRION smiles and says: "yes my dear!!! I too think so."

CAPRION AND VAROCIA both decided to teach MORENA all the tricks and methods related to a warrior. On the other hand, in the palace the training of AAZARO and LAVINZO was started. CAPRION was teaching three of them at different places. MORENA was the best warrior in all of them; she was a great player of swords and arrows. LAVINZO was very good in throwing spears and AAZARO was the best player in swords. The three very special persons were preparing themselves for their future. Only one was there who doesn't wants welfare of ANALASKA and that was LAVINZO. The time passed away the training period was about to be over; when the three magi became 18 years old . . . . they got challenge from their teacher CAPRION. That day CAPRION came to house at noon and silently entered in the room of MORENA, she was cleaning her things when CAPRION attacked on her suddenly and she got some kind of signals and she bended to save herself and replied him in her way; she took out her sword and started fighting with her father, MORENA'S acts and replies were highly crucial and CAPRION noticed that whenever she fights her golden nerves becomes highly virulent and he also felt that whenever she fights, she fights in very aggressive mode. Their fight didn't stop and they fought for two hours and at last CAPRION gave up because he was left with zilch energy and strength. When MORENA won the fight . . . . VAROCIA seeing this fight behind the curtain started clapping for the winner and said, "I told you very earlier my lord that there is one warrior that can defeat you and today she defeated you through your techniques". CAPRION and MORENA chuckled and he said, "My love, I totally agree with you and that's why I tested my lessons that I taught her. My daughter today I am going to give you a challenge that you have to complete, with you two more people are there who will compete with you to complete this task and those are my students like you; I truly want to see that . . . . who is the one whom has grasped my all classes. MORENA took her father's words very seriously and replied," what I have to do?", CAPRION smiled and said," you will be given the map of ANALASKA and in that map five places would be pointed out, you will have to reach at each place and will have to find something. MORENA (in thinking mode)," what I will have to find out?" CAPRION looked his daughter seriously and said," that is the task my daughter, our kingdom is full of powerful souls and astonishing places . . . . you have to find few things which are very essential." MORENA (being in dilemma) said, "What! Are you serious father, I mean our kingdom is full of wonders and I have to find out only the five, why?", CAPRION seeing his daughter so much confused said, "this time only five because your this journey will take minimum four months, the decision is all yours whether you want to join this or not". MORENA sat in front of her father and said in confidence, "father you thought that I deserve this task and you told me everything, this is your faith in me that will help me to reach my destination, I promise you!!!, I will try my level best and will not give up till my last breath". CAPRION hold her daughter and kissed her forehead and said, "Your journey starts from tomorrow". The same words and the same task were given to LAVINZO and AAZARO and these three were preparing for their journey. They did not know that this journey was going to change their lives. That was last night before the journey for those three magi, and they were spending time with their family. VAROCIA was little bit in tension; her heart was not allowing her to send MORENA for this quest . . . . But her mind wanted to see her as a warrior. CAPRION noticed VAROCIA'S this tension while having dinner and they both entered in their room CAPRION tried to make her mood well and said, "the most important thing a warrior should have in it i.e. to survive in all kinds of conditions and to have faith over his confidence, I have seen all this quality in our daughter and I think you have seen the same; don't worry she will come back and you will see her very soon but in other form". Tears came rolling down from VAROCIA'S eyes and she hugged CAPRION. On the other hand, MORENA standing in her balcony was staring the sky, trying to feel less stressed and she was relaxing by taking deep breath and after few minutes she got back to her bed and slept. Again, she saw face of AAZARO but in other manner, she was seeing the moment, when again when she scolded him for the first time and suddenly his face changed; she saw his new face . . . . which appealed to her. MORENA waked up and started whooping, she started talking to herself," who is this guy and what he doing in my dream, huhhh?" She got up from her bed and saw that it was midnight, now she was unable to fall asleep and again she went near to the window and started staring the sky. In the palace someone was there who was unable to sleep and he was also staring the sky same as MORENA and that was AAZARO, he was thinking about her; he still used to think about her mainly as the girl who scolded him very harshly but was very gentle with the injured deer, he was not able to stop thinking about her . . . . he still remembers her and wanted to meet her again; keeping faith on himself and on the words of VAROCIA he had strong confidence that he will meet her again. The next morning these three magi were taking the last knowledge of their journey. CAPRION was teaching MORENA and

LORD NELISH was teaching his boys. They were given the map and the fighting essentials like swords, bows-arrows and spears. When MORENA went in room to meet her parents and to take blessings for the last time before her journey, CAPRION said, "your this map have some secret in itself, you have to reach at these pointed places and have to find the wonders, the paths will play with you, the riddles will make to go in maze and the mystery of wonders will fight with you but you don't have to lose patience, you will have to be very strong, you will have to resolve this and return back as a warrior.", CAPRION handled a very strange type of musical instrument to her and said, "when you will reach at your last thing, you have to blow air in this and the sound of this instrument will come in this kingdom to remind me that you are going to complete your challenge". MORENA took her all the important things and moved for her journey; on the other hand, LORD NELISH was talking his sons and was saying, "I don't know why but CAPRION has selected you both and his one more student to compete with each other and to find out the mystery behind this quest. I hope that you both will try your level best and I wish you all the best for your journey, they both hugged their father and took all the essentials and the same musical instrument as MORENA but of different voice. These magi began with their journey in different directions. The first destination according to the map, for MORENA, AAZARO and LAVINZO was north, west and east points of the jungle respectively.

THE QUEST

By the evening MORENA reached to her first destination but she was not clear with the knowledge that she had to take from there. The night came for magi's and they took rest under the shelter of sky. One week passed away but none of them were getting their ways. When another week started MORENA went near a tree and sat beneath the shelter. She was not able to understand that why she is again coming back to the place from where she started. She concentrated over each and every word of her father and she remembered his words and started talking to herself, "Oh My God!!! How I can be so careless, father told me the paths will play with me, but how can I find a wonder over here; I mean how I can stop this game. Wait! Wait! Wait! These paths are playing with me, so I need to break this chain; I was walking on these paths according to their ways, why should I follow their instructions. Oh My God!!! the first riddle it's all about the decisions of life, we always have to take decisions according to the circumstances around us and we should not follow the path of others or whatever shown by them because a warrior always have to take its own decisions; we can't trust on anyone like these paths which were playing with my mind. Thinking of all these things, MORENA again started her journey and this time she found a hut in the jungle. She entered in the house and said, "Hello! Is anyone there? Hello! Is anyone there?" She suddenly felt that someone is going to attack on her and she bent in front. An old man was there who was attacking on her again but MORENA was not replying to him because he was very old, she hold his hands and said, "Pardon me! But I have not come here to harm you sir". Listening these words from her he stopped and said, "Who are you and why you have come here". MORENA said, "My name is MORENA, I am daughter of the lord of army CAPRION and I have come over here for a quest". "My name is IRISH, I am the oldest foreteller of

ANALASKA and I am going to give you your second challenge" IRISH said. MORENA got amazed and asked, "Second challenge? What was my first challenge?" IRISH chuckled and said, "To come out of the round and playing paths was your first challenge and you did that in much better way". MORENA said, "thank you, so what's going to be my another challenge?", IRISH looked in MORENA'S eyes and said, "just now you are very tired, you have walked a lot, tomorrow we will go for our next challenge". MORENA said, "I don't think that I am tired, I am absolutely fine". IRISH said, "I know you are full of enthusiasm and zest, but this time you need more rest because one by one the tasks will become more crucial and brutal, just have the food and go to bed, there is the room, you can sleep their safely and don't be afraid of me". MORENA said, "I am not. She had the food and went to sleep."

On the other hand, AAZARO and LAVINZO both of them used their brains like MORENA and got out of the jungle, they both also reached a place in the jungle where they found the huts; AAZARO met KEREYON and LAVINZO met LADY DUNNA. They were also told to take rest and become ready for their next task. Next morning they woke up and washed their faces and started doing meditation for their next task. When MORENA and AAZARO were meditating, it was felt by both that they were very close to each other, she saw him and he saw her, both of them remembered their childhood incident. A point came when MORENA got fed up and her meditation got broken up and this thing was noticed by IRISH.

IRISH: "did you see anyone?"

MORENA: "I don't know, I don't know, why these visions like a nightmare don't get out of my mind?"

IRISH: "maybe these visions must be wanting to tell you something it can be both either your future or your past."

MORENA: "I don't know that these visions are essential or not, but they always cross my way."

IRISH looked to her and said," Why you in are trouble my daughter, what's the problem?" MORENA said, "I don't know but only one thing is there i.e. these visions has been following me since my birth."

IRISH: "if you want help I can help you."

MORENA: "How?"

IRISH asked her to sit on the chair and asked her to look in his eyes. IRISH was able to help; he saw a very brutal scene and suddenly moved his face from her. MORENA: "what happen sir what did you see?"

IRISH: "I think it would be better for you to concentrate over your next task these things are worthless and nothing else, forget all the things and let me show you your next task."

After listening such words from IRISH, MORENA didn't have the courage to ask him any question. IRISH took her near his garden and showed her two unicorns, one was in black and other was in white color.

IRISH: "MORENA, you can see these both unicorns, now what you have to do is you have to find which one is biased and which one is unbiased unicorn, among two of them.

MORENA: "What do you mean? How can I judge these both unicorns and how?" IRISH: "this is your only task, I give you two weeks to find out who is the better one, I don't care how you are going to find it out and this is your problem . . . . not mine and this is your second task. Your time starts now."

MORENA took his blessings and held the ropes of the unicorn and moved towards the jungle. On the other hand, AAZARO completely meditated and after his meditation he was very happy because he saw the girl to whom he started loving from her first glance. KEREYON also gave him the same challenge and handled him the two unicorns, AAZARO began with his new task but something else was going on with LAVINZO. LADY DUNNA was not a mere woman, form one touch of the person she was able to tell the character of that person and his intensions. When she saw LAVINZO for the first time . . . . she had slight gasses of his character but she was not all aware. At night when she went to his room, made him to cover him through a blanket, she got in touch with him and suddenly she came in huge stress, she didn't say anything but she decided to tell her these things to LORD NELISH but secretly. She also handled him the same task and he also moved in jungle with those unicorns.

When MORENA went away from the house of IRISH, tears came in his eyes and he said, "pardon me my daughter, pardon me; I was not able to tell you anything, your life is full of curse and pain, you need to survive, someone's else life is dependent on you, you are not a mere woman but a magi who is having her life as a curse, I know no one can escape from their destiny but I will pray to my god to reduce your pain and abolish this immortal curse from you and him. MORENA reached to the midst of the jungle till the evening and AAZARO AND LAVINZO had followed the same path. After LAVINZO left the hut of LADY DUNNA, she wrote a letter to LORD NELISH and said to her white pigeon to deliver this letter to him only. The pigeon went to the palace and left the letter in the room of the LORD NELISH and went away. Unfortunately, JUDASE came to the room of the king for some important work and saw this letter. He picked up the letter and started reading it.

DEAR LORD NELISH,

I WANT TO TELL YOU SOMETHING THAT I NOTICED. YOUR YOUNGER SON LAVINZO IS NOT A HUMAN BUT A PURE EVIL. HE IS NOT SO SIMPLE TO UNDERSTAND AND HE HAS COME TO THIS KINGDOM BECAUSE OF THE BLESSSINGS OF GOD OF HELL "HEAZER". I DON'T KNOW BUT I HAVE GASSED THAT THIS BOY IS THE PRODUCT OF JUDASE WORSHIPS OF HEAZER.

LAST NIGHT WHEN LAVINZO WAS THEIR IN MY HUT, BY CHANCE I TOUCHED HIM AND GOT ALL THE SECRETS BEHIND HIS ENTERANCE IN THIS KINGDOM. I CAN'T WRITE MORE BUT I WANT TO TALK TO YOU; IT'S VERY URGENT. THE END OF HUMANITY HAS BEGUN AND THIS EVIL HAS THE CAPACITY TO EAT THE HUMANITY AND THE PEACE OF OUR KINGDOM. PLEASE MEET ME AS SOON AS POSSIBLE FOR YOU.

YOURS FAITHFULLY
LADY DUNNA

While JUDASE was reading this letter JUBEELIA entered in the room and saw him doing something. JUBEELIA asked, "JUDASE, what are you doing here, do you need something?" JUDASE hiding the letter in his hand and said, "Nothing, actually I came here to meet NELISH; I need to tell him something very important." JUBEELIA said, "Oh! He is there in the garden with ALBERT. They are discussing something about our children." JUDASE said, "Ok! Thank you, I am going to meet him." JUBEELIA found a very different sign on his face, the frown lines on his head was totally visible. JUDASE walked very fast towards his room and locked his room. He murmured in himself, "my god! DUNNA got to know all the secrets, she will tell everything to NELISH; my plans, my dreams, she will ruin everything . . . . I need to do something. I will slave her TODAY." JUDASE came out of his room in hurry and took his horse and went to his way. He reached to her hut till the evening. He entered in hut, LADY DUNNA was making something; she heard the sound of the entrance of JUDASE and said, "Welcome JUDASE! I know for what you have come here. Don't feel bad just perform your task. JUDASE in anger said, "You know what, I have come here to kill you. But you are wrong this time . . . . your prediction is wrong. You know what type of qualities I possess for my enemies, I don't slave them but, ha ha-ha!!!" LADY DUNNA in perturbed way asked, "what are your intentions JUDASE?," JUDASE stopped laughing, he holds her neck and pointed knife towards her and says, "my intention is to abolish all the people who comes in my way, my intention is to own this kingdom and spread the evil powers all over, my intension is to rule humanity by evil and my intention is to vanish people like you who tries to ruin my dreams. LADY DUNNA in cursing manner said, "whatever you are thinking is not going to happen and if you do so then note my words, like your evil messenger, great warriors and savior of humanity has also taken birth, he will abolish your thoughts, he will never ever let your dreams come true, he will be around you and his beloved will kill you, both of them have taken birth JUDASE. It's not the end of humanity but the beginning of new lesson. Whatever you are doing with your brother, someone else will come in your evil empire who is going to have immense power of evils but he will deceive you, like you are doing, you betrayer. Always remember the history is very crucial and it repeats itself." JUDASE threw her on the floor and hypnotizes her and says, "LADY DUNNA from now onwards you will work for me and you don't know anything about me or LAVINZO." LADY DUNNA was hypnotized by him and she started working for him. After completing his work, JUDASE came back to the palace and went to his room. Meanwhile, the magi were not able to find the ways for the answer of this riddle. 13 days passed away and only LAVINZO was able to find the answer and he moved for his third task, he went to LADY DUNNA's hut and handled the unicorn, she gave him the unicorn of his wish and went inside to the hut. Here MORENA and AAZARO were working together, she again went in the groove of the tree and remembers the words of CAPRION, she remembers that he told her that the riddles will take her in maze, and then she did a very different thing and found her answer; the same thing was performed by AAZARO, it felt that they both were connected with their minds and hearts both. The day when the second week was going to be over AAZARO and MORENA reached at their destinations. MORENA again went to IRISH's hut and AAZARO also went back to KEREYON's hut. She handled him both the unicorns and said, "This black unicorn is the perfect and unbiased one". IRISH was shocked and said, "how did you find this?", MORENA smiled and said, "within two weeks I tried to make friendly and good relations with both of them and did all the things that were required but one day when I was not able to find food for them and suddenly few bandit types guys attacked on me . . . . then only this black unicorn helped me, he didn't take the revenge from me for his food as this white unicorn did and I found my answer; the color, the race and the belongings of anyone whether it is a human or an animal can't allow a person to judge him on these basis but our deeds, our sacrifices and a feeling of overwhelming can only be the things that allows us to judge him and help us to take our decisions. The loyalty of a person can only help a warrior to trust him." After listening the words of MORENA, IRISH was quite shocked. He had the feeling that she would choose the white unicorn but she took the right decision and in this happiness he spoke few words for her in revere, "I met many people who defines a person on the basis of the things you said, but only you . . . . who was able to find the answer of this task in a very simplest manner, your parents will be proud of themselves that they have given birth a daughter like you." MORENA smiled and took his permission for leaving. IRISH being so happy from her . . . . asked her to take her loyal fellow the black unicorn.

MORENA: "Why are you giving me this?"

IRISH: "I have lost my all the rights on him because now he has got too much love from you and want to support you in your this journey. Please don't say no for him, this is my request."

MORENA took IRISH's blessings and moved to the jungle for her next task again. The same condition was there with AAZARO, he also handled the unicorns and told KEREYON who is the perfect, but he got the white female unicorn from him and he also moved towards the jungle for his next task. The next task was quite different from other tasks and in this task two magi have to be together. MORENA was walking in the jungle and talking to the unicorn, "hey! From now onwards your name is ALMAS and I will call you that." The unicorn replied her by moving his head. AAZARO named his unicorn RUBIZN and was very happy after talking to her. Meanwhile, something else was going on in the mind of LAVINZO and he decided to leave this challenge and started moving in jungle where ever he wanted to go. The third task was to learn the method of tracking the attack through ears, when you are blind and you are not able to see but you have to keep patience and need to learn the method of this thing. Both of them, MORENA and AAZARO were at their paths except LAVINZO. That day only MORENA and AAZARO met their teachers, the tribes of the kingdom who only lives in the jungle but they all respect the people as well as the king of the kingdom. KYRA was the teacher of AAZARO who was herself blind and crippled by one leg, MORENA met NISUS who was also blind and the creator of this lesson. They both were welcomed in a very lavish manner at different places. From the next morning, they both began with their practice. Three weeks passed away now .... MORENA and AAZARO were ready with their lessons and to meet each other. NISUS asked MORENA, "I have given you all the knowledge of this thing .... but your task begins here, you have to prove that you have grasped the knowledge of my lessons". MORENA: "What I have to do my lord?"

NISUS: "You have to fight with a student of my wife KYRA through the methods I taught you."

MORENA: "I respect your words my lord, I will surely fight and also I will try to win."

NISUS: "this is the only thing in you that allowed me teach your simplicity, patience, fullness and calmness. Mainly your confidence on yourself always helped you to reach at your destinations; you don't have the greed of winning this task but have the greed to get the knowledge." . . . .

MORENA had click smile on her face and said, "knowledge is the most important thing, without that I am nothing and I don't have the greed of being a winner because loss and gain is part of life like the two sides of a river and one always should have the feeling of avarice for knowledge . . . ."

NISUS: "Such attitude and greatness are the symbol of a great warrior." . . . . They both chuckled and NISUS asked MORENA to get ready for the fight tonight. On the other hand, the same words were told to AAZARO by KYRA and he was also asked to get ready for tonight. The magi were unaware that they are going to meet after so many years. They both got ready in their dresses; it was a rule that if a girl is fighting against a boy then she has to hide her face through the stole. NISUS and KYRA helped these both magi to get ready. The ground was covered with bamboos, the ground was full of mud and fire was all over there. That night seemed as if it's going to choose its perfect warrior. They both came in the ring, there was innocent silence. Neither MORENA nor AAZARO recognized each other but the time had come to face each other. Having sword in hands, NISUS and KYRA tied a piece of cloth in their eyes. They both got MORENA and AAZARO in the middle of the ring. KYRA ringed the bell and the fight started. They both had to attack on the each other by listening the sounds of the swords. They both were fighting like true warriors and none of them were giving up. All of a sudden, the fire of the ring reached at its apex and caught the clothes of the tents, no one noticed this thing till the fire burnt the one tent; MORENA attacked very brutally on AAZARO and while attacking him she heard the voice of a baby who was there in the burning tent and got distracted, AAZARO took this advantage and attacked her due to which her sword fell off and so was she.

They both removed their eye patches and by mistake MORENA removed her stole from her face. AAZARO saw her face and got lost somewhere, he was lost in her so deeply that he was took away his sword from her neck. MORENA pushed his sword through his hands and ran away to save that child. When everyone saw her running they turned back and started shouting, some of them were getting water, some of them were trying to save others but MORENA was the only one who used her lessons properly. She entered in the tent somehow and took the baby from cradle, covered him in her dress and came out of it. He was the youngest baby to whom she saved and gave him to his parents. Seeing this unfortunate courage of MORENA . . . . AAZARO, KYRA, NISUS and every one of the tribe saluted her. MORENA saw very different type of respect in the eyes of the people around her. AAZARO came in front and bent down on his knees with the sword and said, "You are the real winner of this task miss MORENA." He was looking at her like an innocent child who stares at the sweets with greediness. MORENA looked in front of all the people and said, "whatever I did is nothing, it was my duty and responsibility and I don't deserve this respect, the real and true winner is AAZARO; it matters hardly that I saved a soul, it's not important . . . . But the most important thing is this that I lost my concentration and I lost the challenge too." She comes near to NISUS and said, "Kindly pardon me, my sir, my lord; I didn't stand at your faith but I promise I will continue my practice and one day will get perfection on this." Tears came in the eyes of NISUS and he said, "My daughter whatever I taught you, you didn't only performed that but you showed that really someone's life and soul is more important than any winnings. I am proud of you and I fell proud on myself too because I taught your kind of student." Everyone near them started cheering and they made a huge celebration. One thing was missing in the ceremony that was MORENA and AAZARO was searching for her. After few minutes someone came near to him and told him that MORENA's hand was slightly burnt and she has gone to take medicine. AAZARO after hearing all this got calmness and also got lost in her thoughts. He was remembering their first meeting; it was quite surprising to know that he recognized where she didn't. He was lost in her dark blue eyes, in her long wavy hair, in her rosy pink lips, in her childish innocent face and in her golden shinning body. He was not able to come out of his thoughts and saw MORENA coming near to him.

MORENA: "Congratulations! You won the task."

AAZARO: "PLEASE! Don't make me feel ashamed on myself."

MORENA: "why would I do that? You won the challenge and you are the winner."

AAZARO: "can you see everyone now?"

MORENA: "YES!!!!"

AAZARO: "Then see them very carefully and me too . . . . we all are celebrating in your honor, it's not about winning or losing . . . . it's all about the exact quality of a warrior and you have all the things that define you as a great warrior."

MORENA: "Now please stop flattering."

AAZARO: "I am standing on the floor of flattering but telling you the truth. Ok, now let's talk about something else; do you remember that we have met earlier too?"

MORENA: "earlier? I don't remember any such incident."

AAZARO: "but I still remember everything . . . . your kindness, your royalty and your scolding's.", Listening the words scolding she looked in his eyes and got reminded about their first meeting and said, "Oh My god!!! You ah, can't believe; you still remember that incident?"

AAZARO: "when I didn't allowed your essence to go away from me than how can I allow you to go out of me."

A feeling of shyness came inside her. AAZARO asked, "Are you on this quest too?" MORENA replied, "Yes, I am the student as well as the daughter of SIR CAPRION and he has sent me over here." Then, AAZARO said that he has sent me too, means you are his third student. MORENA said, "YES, do you have any doubt?"

AAZARO: "No, I don't have any doubt at least not now." . . . . Eventually, NISUS and KYRA came near to both of them and said, "Enjoy the celebration children because tomorrow you both have to continue your journey together." MORENA and AAZARO spoke together, "together! But why?"

NISUS: "Because this was last part of alone journey and the rest two challenges have to be completed together. I thought that I will be teaching LAVINZO and AAZARO, because I was not sure about you. You through your patience and courage won this task and I hope that you both are going to have great knowledge through this journey." AAZARO and MORENA enjoyed the celebration and next morning they got ready for their journey. Before leaving from there, MORENA went to the hut of NISUS where he was seeing his secret box. MORENA asked, "Can I come in sir?" NISUS replied, "Yes! My daughter, come in. MORENA asked, "What is this?" NISUS said, "It is my secret box, which I am opening after so many years." MORENA said, "I thought you are blind by birth.", NISUS chuckled and said, "seeing my condition . . . . No one can predict that I was able to see this world once. I was also like a warrior like you but a time came when I lost my eyes while fighting with enemies of our kingdom and in order to save me KYRA also I became like this, but I didn't feel bad neither she; at that time only I and she together introduced this kind of fighting knowledge. We practiced a lot and we accomplished this knowledge through our hard work. Seeing our patience and devotion towards our kingdom, GOD ARMMANDO blessed us through this pious piece of cloth and he said, "Whenever you find your qualities in someone else than give this clothe to him or her, he or she will be your mirror image. Today I saw me in yourself and I give this to you." MORENA said, "how can I accept this, you are the real owner of this pious cloth." NISUS kept that piece of cloth in her hands and said "take care my daughter and always remain same." . . . . After saying these words NISUS came out of the hut with her. Outside the hut AAZARO was waiting for her with both the unicorns, they both took the blessings of the people and moved for their next task. They both again went to the jungle for their task. AAZARO and MORENA had a glance over their maps and found NISUS words were right. They saw that they both have to visit a cave which was in the north direction of the jungle. They both moved to the same direction and introduced their selves.

MORENA: "so, you are here because of the order of your parents?"

AAZARO: "actually, no, I am here because I wanted to utilize the knowledge that I got from my teacher and you?"

MORENA: "same here."

AAZARO: "great!!! By the way this quest is really very lucky for me."

MORENA: "why?"

AAZARO: "because of this quest I met you and at least after so many years I will be able to ask you for your forgiveness."

MORENA: "my forgiveness?"

AAZARO: "you must have forgotten that incident, but that incident changed my life, you taught me to respect the life of everyone whether it's human or an animal. From then only I wanted to meet you but you were lost somewhere, even the airs and this mud were so angry with me that they were not telling anything about you; your foot prints were abolished and your smell was also getting away from me but see even the god gave me one chance, now can I ask you for your forgiveness."

MORENA smiled with shy and said, "realizing the mistake only can forgive you and it's not important that I should forgive you but a human is able to forgive himself with the feelings of regret . . . . then even god forgives him, so who I am to forgive you?", AAZARO with a smile said, "has anyone told you?"

MORENA: "What?"

AAZARO: "each word that comes out of your mouth . . . . can win anyone's heart." MORENA: "you are quite amusing and a very good flatterer."

AAZARO: "maybe . . . . but miss I am the prince of the kingdom, why I need to be flatterer."

MORENA didn't have any answer and she got slight signals of AAZARO's feelings. They both walked very far but didn't get the right path, the night came and they settled down under groove of a big tree. They ate some berries and few fruits and slept. At mid night AAZARO woke up and saw MORENA standing near ALMAS. AAZARO: "what are you doing here? I thought you must be sleeping."

MORENA: "I was sleeping but the nightmares and the bad visions always wake me up."

AAZARO: "visions! What kind of visions you are talking about?"

MORENA: "from my birth . . . . till yet I see something but don't understand why I am seeing it and this vicious visions are very scary."

AAZARO: "when I used to see the nightmares I usually go to the room of my mother and tell her everything and she asked me to pray to GOD ARMMANDO, he will take my all the nightmares; in her front I join my hand and just think of our god and suddenly my fears, they just go out of me.", MORENA smiled and said, "I know what you meant to say. Ok! Let me do like you do." She closed her eyes and concentrated to god ARMMANDO, But immediately she opened her eyes and said, "you just don't bother and go back to sleep, I will be fine." After saying these words she went back to her place again turned her face, so that AAZARO can't see her. AAZARO also came back to his place but didn't sleep for the whole night he was staring her with some strange feelings. He didn't have any idea that slowly and gradually he was falling in love with her. The next morning when he woke up he didn't find MORENA at her place, a vicious feeling came in his heart and he started searching for her. Walking on the paths he reached to a place where there was a sacred pond, he found her clothes lying at the mud; but not all the cloths were there, he turned his face at the right side and saw that near the water fall MORENA was bathing. He did hide out his face but wasn't able to control him through watching this but then also he didn't see anything and when he saw that she is returning, he went back to his place, acting like a sleeping boy. MORENA came near to him and started waking him up.

MORENA: "AAZARO, wake up, we have to move." Few drops of water of her hairs fell on his face and he woke up.

AAZARO: "You have taken bath?"

MORENA: "I have the habit of waking up early in the morning, now just wake up and walk for few miles, there is a sacred pond; you can take bath and just get some food.",

After saying these words she went to search for food, but AAZARO was like in unconscious mood, he swept the water from his face and smelled it and said, "You still bear the fragrance." He also got up and took bath. MORENA got few apples from the jungle and said, "I can't find better food for us."

AAZARO: "at least it's better than the raw food."

They both laughed and started their journey again. Just like the last day they didn't find their way but after few weeks passed they saw a cave, a very strange cave. They entered in it and saw obscure things around them, outside the cave there was light and heat but inside the cave there was coldness. MORENA and AAZARO noticed the wall they saw bodies of people which were freezed in the ice. AAZARO eyes went on a shining thing, he left MORENA and went near to that thing, and it was nothing but a beautiful golden flute. He took it up and had a closed look to it. While AAZARO was doing this, MORENA turned at her left hand side and saw the spirits of evils, giants and ghosts which were freezed too. She saw that just under these things something was written, MORENA read that out and it was written;

PLAY THE FLUTE, BLOW AIR IN IT, LET THE DOORS OF TWO FACES OPENS, THE MORTALS AND IMMORTALS GOES IN IT'S KINGDOM, ALL WE NEED IS VERY MERE, THE KIND AND GENEROUS HIS EYES EVERYWHERE, DON'T STOP THE LUDICURUS TUNE OTHERWISE THE DARK MOON WILL RISE VERY SOON.

While MORENA was reading this riddle AAZARO played the flute and a heart piercing tune came out of it. MORENA was shocked and she shouted, "AAZARO don't you stop playing the flute if you do so then these giants and ghosts will come out of the ice. Just play the flute and let the tune comes out of it till these pious souls get released from here." AAZARO through his last lesson heard everything said by her. While he was playing the flute the ice of the pious and good souls melted and they both saw two doors opening just behind them, one door was the path of heaven and other was the path of hell. These pious souls were taking the path of heaven by themselves. Again MORENA noticed the area where this riddle was written, she saw that the riddle was changed and this time something else was written in it.

REACHING TO THE DESTINATION IS NOT SO MERE, YOU HAVE RAGED HIS ANGER ONCE AGAIN, NOW HELP THE WARRIOR IF YOU CAN BECAUSE I AM GOING TO SHOW WHAT I AM.

On the other hand, from where the pious souls were getting released a soul came near to MORENA and said, "you have done something that can even take your life and I can't see that, so just listen to me, use your sword as much as you can in order to destroy these giants and to save your fellow, don't let him stop this tune if he do so then the only one door will remain open i.e. the hell. Walk like a warrior and only follow the path of air, don't you dare to turn away because it will harm you in all its way." After saying such words the soul also followed its path and went away. Suddenly, MORENA herd the voices of giants, she saw the ice cracking and the evils came out. MORENA took her sword out and started fighting with them. Screaming, groaning and the grunts. AAZARO was able to see everything but he was helpless, he has to do his work. AAZARO saw the number of the evils was increasing and he thought, MORENA might not be able to fight with all these giants but he was not able to do anything. Then MORENA saw an evil attacking AAZARO, he attacked on him through his sword, MORENA ran and killed that evil and AAZARO didn't stop playing the flute. All the pious souls reached at their destinations and the door of heaven got closed, then the door of hell spread a red spark outside and got all the evil spirits and both the doors got closed. AAZARO fell down and MORENA realized that that sword was poisonous; she kept his head in her lap and took out the sacred piece of cloth that NISUS gave her and tied it on his wounded hand. AAZARO didn't open his eyes but he was breathing. MORENA didn't understand why . . . . But tears came in her eyes and she hugged him for the first time. She kept his head on the floor and came out of the cave. Taking ALMAS from there she went to IRISH hut again. ALMAS took her to his hut within few minutes, she made ALMAS to stand out and went inside the hut and shouted, "IRISH, IRISH, IRISH . . . , where are you?", Listening such pain full voice IRISH came out of his secret room and sees MORENA standing in his front. MORENA said, "IRISH, help me, the evils attacked on." Before she tells the rest to him he said, "This is the natural medicine I have, this will cure your partner. Don't panics, your piece of cloth has cured him half and now go and cure him fully." MORENA took the medicine and sat on ALMAS, with the feeling of thankfulness in her eyes for IRISH . . . . she went off. She reached in the cave again and saw AAZARO groaning in pain, his eyes were searching her and she reached their and again kept his head in her lap and made him to take the medicine.

AAZARO (in pain): "I thought you are gone and left me on my condition." MORENA (having tears in her eyes): "no AAZARO, it's not possible; this was the only theory of this challenge; to trust your partner and have faith in them, also support in every manner in which you can and you believed me, showed your faith in me, you didn't stop till our task got over, I am so proud of you AAZARO as being your partner in this journey."

AAZARO (groaning in pain): "I think I am better now."

MORENA: "No you can't be better, you need to take rest and only one challenge is left, so we have enough time left with us."

AAZARO (with a click smile): "remember I told you earlier, your words can win anyone's heart and today they took my pain." Again MORENA felt shy but she didn't show it. They both took rest in that cave only for that night. Morning came with shinning bright sun, this time AAZARO woke up first and staring MORENA, the bright sunrays were disturbing her; he picked his wounded hand to give her shadow, after few minutes she woke up and saw what AAZARO was doing, she was quite surprise and saw his wounded hand.

MORENA: "are you an imbecile or something else, you are hurt and raised your wounded hand, why? What was the need?".

AAZARO: "I don't know, it doesn't pain at all; actually you were getting disturbed by these rays so I was just giving the shadow to your eyes. The beautiful blue ocean eyes."

MORENA (in dilemma): "let me see the wound!!!" She opened the cloth and said, "It's perfect, I mean your wound has recovered a lot, this sacred cloth really worked, I think now we both can move for our next task.

AAZARO: "Yes! Definitely we can move, I think we should move."

They both came out of the cave and moved for their last task of the journey. The last task theory was quite different from the previous tasks. They both reached at place according to the map where peoples were there and they were quite scared. They came down from their unicorns, a little boy was hiding near the bushes; MORENA looked at him and held his hand, the little boy started crying, "leave me, I haven't done anything; don't kill me please." MORENA held him and said, "Sorry! I didn't mean to hurt, but why are you so scared, what's the problem?" The boy replied, "You must be from his side and have come here to kill me because I am only rest".

MORENA: "who is he and you are only rest what do you mean by that?"

The boy said, "You don't know about him." AAZARO (showing feeling of comfortableness) asked, "we don't know anything that you are talking about and what is your name?, where are all the people gone." The boy replied, "My name is AZEN and all the people of this area have not gone anywhere but they are hiding themselves because some of very different creatures comes to our area and takes one child every week from our area."

MORENA: "why they come over here and what they do with the children?" The boy replied, "We are their food, and they eat us." AAZARO asked, "Why didn't you tell your king about whatever happening here?" The boy said, "They watch us out every time and because of their carefulness we are unable to do anything. But who are you and why you have come here?" MORENA said her words with sympathy and calmness, "don't worry we are here to save you all and we promise we will abolish their fear from your hearts." All the people of the area they came out and asked both of them for their help.

AAZARO: "firstly, tell me what is going on here and who is this giant about whom he was talking."

AZEN: "he doesn't belong to anyone but he has a team of evils, they come over here at every 7th day and picks a child and take that child away; till now they have taken more than 30 children and now I am only left that's why I was hiding myself from you both." An old man came out of the mob and said, "My name is TRILOG and I know how you can kill them."

MORENA: "Tell us how this can be done?"

AAZARO: "Are they something else, can't they be killed through our swords?", TRILOG: "no, not at all, they are highly powered evils and giants and they can only be killed through a special sword and that sword is kept in the cave where they reside but reaching near the sword is quite impossible."

MORENA: "everything is possible in our lives, only the greed is necessary."

TRILOG: "good, I wanted to hear this thing only, now listen there is a cave inside the waterfall and you have to enter in it, don't try to move in front of them because they are unable to notice anyone at night but if you move they will kill you. The sword is inserted in a rock but if you reach over their you won't be having any kind of problem but when one of you will take out the sword . . . . from there the evils themselves will get to know and they will attack on you, the normal evils can be killed by both of you but the one who eats us will only be killed by one of you . . . . who will take out the sword."

MORENA: "AZEN, do you know the path?"

AZEN: "Yes, I know the path!!"

AAZARO: "then we just shouldn't wait anymore and AZEN . . . . you only show the path to us." AZEN said, "OK!!!" The three took the path and AZEN showed them their way. They reached near the waterfall.

AZEN: "my responsibility was still here and can't help you anymore. Now you need to help me out because tomorrow is the seventh day and I am the only child in my group." He joined his hands and said, "Please!!! Save my life; I don't want to die now. MORENA held his hands and said, "we are not goanna let anybody hurt you; just believe in us . . . . we will help you in all the manners, in which we can.

AZEN: "you both know, you making your life to get in risk because of me." AAZARO: "no, my child, nothing is like that, this is our duty, our responsibility and let me know you one thing, and the most important quality of a warrior is that he/she is the savior."

AZEN: "its twilight now, after few hours you both can enter in this water fall and please stay away from their swords, their swords are highly poisonous; only one cut and you are finished. So, please take care and hoping for the best outcomes." After wishing them AZEN moved towards his path. They both were waiting for the night and the night came very fast. It was full moon night and they entered inside the waterfall. It was a quite surprising cave; graveyard like silence was there at that place. Many a times they both met the evils but they used to stop moving and the evils didn't understand about them. TRILOG had already told them that they shouldn't get lost in the labyrinth of the paths; they should only follow the path that they think is highly silenced. There were so many paths and AAZARO depicted the right path. They were walking silently and suddenly they saw the shinning silver sword. That sword was really inserted in the rock and it was a quite different sword.

MORENA: "Just go AAZARO, don't wait, I am here to welcome the evils." AAZARO: "Ok!!"

AAZARO gets near to the rock and applies the force on the sword . . . . But it was not coming out of the rock, MORENA sees him and she gets close to him to help him. Now, they both apply force on the sword and it comes out. For fraction of seconds it was felt that everything is fine.

AAZARO: "I think no one is goanna come here, TRILOG may be a fool."

MORENA: "No, this silence is saying something, it's not the end . . . . it is the beginning of something."

AAZARO: "what do you mean by that?"

MORENA: "when the ocean stops its tides and disasters' it doesn't mean that it is the end, actually it's the beginning of the end." As she said these words, the evils from all the corners of the cave started coming to them and the fight began. AAZARO shouted, "MORENA, don't let them hurt you, their swords are highly poisoned." And, eventually they both killed all the evils and unfortunately the cave started shivering. The full moon got covered with black clouds and suddenly everything stopped. More evils in comparison to earlier come for fight, it was not looking like a fight but it was like a war. Behind AAZARO, the rock from where they took out the sword . . . . turned into one eye and that rock came out in the form of a shouting and roaring giant evil.

MORENA: "KREYEATH, it's him."

AAZARO (shouting in dilemma): "KREYEATH, who is he?"

MORENA (replied in high pitch voice): "TRILOG told me about him, he is the only evil that can be killed through this sword."

AAZARO: "but how? He is very big?"

MORENA: "he is unable to watch us now . . . . just don't move in his front and when he looks at somewhere else . . . . Then attack him at five different places, I am taking care of these evils and you take care of him." . . . .

They both started with their wise mind. They were not moving in front of them but killing them with their minds. AAZARO attacked KREYEATH four times at four different places, it was felt that they are going to win this and only one time was left. Unfortunately, something wrong happened while attacking on the evils one of them saw AAZARO and went to insert his poisonous sword in his back but MORENA noticed it and she came in front of AAZARO. Though, she was wounded, she killed him. She was breathing very fast and seeing AAZARO. AAZARO attacked on that giant evil for the last time but he didn't die. Then he remembered that this giant can only be killed through a person who takes out this sword from his eyes and they both took out this sword together.

AAZARO (shouting in pain) said, "MORENA!! I need you, he can only be killed from both of us, and I can't make it alone." He saw her groaning and not speaking anything then he thought of something. AAZARO ran towards her in front of KREYEATH to make him noticed by KREYEATH. He noticed him running and he roars. AAZARO reached to her and supported her to stand then they both held the sword and KREYEATH attacked on them by his hand. AAZARO and MORENA simply held their sword and inserted it in his palm and then took out the sword from his palm. The giant evil started groaning in pain and his whole body turned into ashes and fell down on the floor. MORENA fell down again . . . . AAZARO touched her body it was turning to blue and was getting cold. He took her in his arms and came out of the cave. After he came out the cave, the cave itself went inside the land. He kept her on his unicorn and with ALMAS and RUBIZN he moved back to that area again. She was kept on RUBIZN and ALMAS was trying to move her through his head, he was again and again using his head to lift her hands . . . . but no response was coming. Tears came out from his eyes and he stopped doing so. AAZARO with all of them reached to that area again, the people of that area came out, and AAZARO saw AZEN coming towards MORENA. He looked her, touched her face and started crying. AAZARO approached to TRILOG, he joined his hands and says, "Please save her!!! Because of me she is in this condition, save her." TRILOG conducting his mob, "all the women took MORENA in the room. She was kept on the bed and prayers started. After few hours TRILOG came out of the room and talks to AAZARO.

TRILOG: "the extreme poison has spread in her whole body, her nerves speed is very low, her body temperature is coming down and she is still breathing very fast, it seems to me that she is taking her last breath. She can't be cured, pardon me!!", Saying these words TRILOG started walking towards his hut and suddenly AAZARO shouts, "she can't die, I have not permitted her, and I have not allowed her to leave me like this. She can't die TRILOG just take care of her, she can't die."

TRILOG: "she didn't come to your life because of your permission; she has to face her destiny."

AAZARO: "the destiny, the god and all the immortal things around me can't break my hope, till the time I am breathing she will also breathe and when this one heart stops beating the other one will be stopped by itself."

TRILOG: "I respect your feelings AAZARO but I am helpless I can't do anything, she can't be saved, and her each crucial heart beat is taking her near to her death." AAZARO holds the shirt of TRILOG and says, "I am not standing in a cave TRILOG where only a ray of hope can come . . . . I am standing on the land with open wide sky where the rays of hope are immense and my heart can't tell a lie to me. Just take care of her." TRILOG didn't respond on this rude behavior of AAZARO, he truly understood the feelings of AAZARO. Even AAZARO was not understanding why it was happening with him, what feelings pierced his heart; he was in love with an unknown face. Days passed away but MORENA was lying on the bed like that, no better condition was there, AAZARO was not eating the food since the day she fell down, day-by-day his condition was also going down and one day a messenger god reached to that place. It was IRISH, he was aware of all the incidents. He went near to AAZARO and said, "I can save her, don't worry she will be fine, her work has not finished yet and before the accomplishment of our work in this world we can't go near to our god."

AAZARO: "do whatever you want and if you need then take my life, I will not mind it at all but save her, please!!"

IRISH: "you're this patience and your unbreakable trust pulled me here; give that sacred piece of cloth that she tied on your hand to save you." AAZARO opened that sacred cloth from his hand and gave that to IRISH, he took the sacred cloth to the hut where MORENA was lying in deep sleep, and IRISH tied the cloth on her and had a glance over her face. He talked to her by saying, "my daughter, this is the reason why I didn't tell you about your nightmares, those are not very kind but very crucial, this is the only beginning, and your destiny wants something very harsh from you. He touched her face and tears came from his eyes." He came out of the hut and said to AAZARO, "I have done for what I came here, now just pray to your god to show his mercy on her, the pious cloth will mitigate her poison but ask your god to show his mercy on her for once.", After saying these words IRISH went away. AAZARO came to the hut and stares at her and says, "what I should call you, my heart, my patience, my breath or my life, I don't know but only one thing I want from you please come back, don't leave me like this." He holds her hand and then says, "MORENA you never asked me that how I recognized you after so long time, you know I never forgot you, I didn't let my heart to think of anyone else neither my heart tried to do so by itself. When you got hurt by that attack . . . . I felt your pain in me, I was helpless but not a coward and if you didn't wake up then I will feel like a coward, I know you will never let me feel so, I know you will come back, you have to return for me because I love you, I love you and I can't let my love to leave me like this; please don't do this to me, don't be so brutal towards me please, I beg you!!!!!", He was hiding his tears and his hopeful eyes didn't allow his tears to come out. He came out of the hut and sat near the tree. On the other hand, MORENA's life was coming back. When AZEN went to her hut he saw MORENA opening her pearl eyes. AZEN (came near to the bed and supports her to sit): "MORENA you came back, AAZARO was right; you won the battle of your life." AZEN came out of the hut screaming, "MORENA is back!!!!, AAZARO!!!!, MORENA is back!!!!; she won the battle!!!!!!", AAZARO listened the words of AZEN and he ran like air, he entered in the hut and hugged her so tightly as if he will not let her go anywhere, MORENA also held him and AAZARO kissed her forehead and said, "you came back, I was right, my heart was right, you are back." That day for the first time tears came out of his eyes and he hugged her again. MORENA was not sure about the feelings of AAZARO and AAZARO also did not tell her anything. Suddenly, all the people gathered in the room of her and TRILOG said," welcome MORENA, WELCOME TO YOUR NEW LIFE!!!!!" The journey of this quest for both of you ends here. You both achieved the things for what you came over here, now you both possess the quality of a great warrior, here is the instrument . . . . now blow air in this to tell the whole ANALASKA that you both have achieved your goal. AAZARO took his and MORENA's equipment and blew air in it, the sound was heard by all the people of ANALASKA. LISTENING the echoing sound, the king and CAPRION got the news of the quest . . . . They both got to know that MORENA and AAZARO have completed their task. LORD NELISH again announced to his mob about the ceremony of the next king of ANALASKA, he wanted to celebrate the day when AAZARO was going to return to his home. That beautiful night, celebration was also made in the area where AAZARO and MORENA were there. The next morning they took the permission from everyone and moved to their houses. Before they began to move TRILOG told AAZARO to take care of her and said, "She is not totally fine, it will take a long time for her to heal completely, so take care of her." AAZARO promises to take care of her and then they leave that area. After they went away from that area, AZEN asked TRILOG.

AZEN: "TRILOG I didn't see AAZARO having tears in his eyes when MORENA was sick but he cried on the day when she got up from her deep sleep, why?",

TRILOG: "My dear AZEN, AAZARO didn't cry at that time because a pain of losing love was stopping him to do so . . . . But he didn't let his tears to come out and when he saw his love getting back to him then the pain of losing her, got out of his eyes. The pain of separation is very crucial; it takes the reason from us to live. AAZARO was not thinking that MORENA was near to death but he was seeing his life going near to death.",

AZEN: "that means AAZARO loves her? ",

TRILOG: "loves her?, he dies for her, for her only he stopped eating food, for her only he changed to theist from atheist; he truly loves her, even he doesn't know about the deepest feeling of his love growing in his heart for her."

AZEN: "Will MORENA also goanna fall in love with him?"

TRILOG: "I am a mere human not a foreteller."

They both laughed and stopped their discussion. On the other hand, AAZARO and MORENA were at the midst of the jungle. AAZARO seeing condition of MORENA asked her to take rest and she agreed. They went near a pond and sat under the groove of tree.

AAZARO: "are you feeling good now?"

MORENA: "yes! I am totally fine."

AAZARO: "then why are you whooping?"

MORENA: "actually, yesterday I woke up from the deepest sleep, may be because of that I am not feeling enthusiastic."

AAZARO: "we are not in rush, our journey of the quest has ended and we can now go to our kingdom, so what's the need to go in hurry, just be relax this time, you will be safe with me."

MORENA: "I know with you no one can harm me but I really don't know why I am feeling drowsy and sleepy."

AAZARO: "It is because you are not totally well and you need to take more rest, TRILOG has informed me about your condition; just do one thing you sleep here for a while.",

MORENA: "yes, I do need this sleep." .... MORENA slept down and AAZARO started talking to ALMAS and RUBIZN.

AAZARO: "ALMAS do me a favor, can you please get some fresh fruits for her because I can't leave her alone here."

ALMAS moved his head and went to the jungle in search of food. MORENA was taking rest and AAZARO was keeping his eyes on her. It was felt that he was blinking his eyes very less. He was staring her like anything. The evening came and MORENA got up, she noticed AAZARO keeping his eyes on her. MORENA gave a very click smile to him. She looked up and saw that she has slept for a long time. MORENA: "I think I slept for a long time, the evening has arrived."

AAZARO: "I want to show you something."

MORENA: "What?"

AAZARO came near to her and held her hands, helped her to stand and they both moved near the edge of the pond. MORENA saw the half visible sun, the atmosphere around her was very pink, the flowers and the leaves were blooming, the water had the shade of the golden and red colors; and the most unbelievable thing in the wide blue sky was the rainbow which was showing its all 7 colors. MORENA: "it's beautiful; I mean it's amazing, I have never ever seen such astonishing things together."

AAZARO: "it's not the first time for me, after our first meeting I usually come to this part of jungle to see the real and pious beauty." While saying these words AAZARO's eyes got stuck on her face. MORENA too was not able to see anywhere else except him, while seeing each other they came closer, closer and closer. They came very close, AAZARO held her and she also fallen down in some other feelings. They both moved for their first kiss. They were kissing and they were very close.

When they were kissing the thunders shouted, black clouds covered the bright colors and it started raining. When she heard the shouting thunders, they both stopped and she hugged him saying, "I am afraid of these thunders." While holding her in his arms he said, "With me you don't have to worry, I am always there for you." It started raining heavily and MORENA realized that what she has done. She left him like anything and moved back. This time she was unable to face AAZARO and she ran away. AAZARO didn't understand why she did that, but a feeling of love told everything to him. MORENA went near to ALMAS and sat down over there. On the other hand, IRISH listened the shouting and roaring thunders and he got know that what it is symbolizing, he spoke to himself, "these thunders and these vicious clouds have covered the bright future of someone, the beginning of the end has begun." Suddenly the rain stopped and MORENA came near to AAZARO again but this time she was reacting in some other way, AAZARO and MORENA were trying to convince them that nothing has happened, they started behaving like strangers. The night came and they both fallen down in deep sleep. MORENA was twisting and turning, it felt that she is watching some very vicious nightmare. In her nightmare she saw AAZARO, she began to run in order to hug him but before she reached, A GIANT man killed him with his thunder powers and she shouted very loudly, "noooooooooooooooooo!!!!!!" and suddenly she woke up; she started whooping. Listening this loud voice of her AAZARO woke up.

AAZARO: "MORENA, what happened?, did you see that nightmare again?, Is everything fine?", Seeing AAZARO being stressed out she said, "no I am fine, everything is all right". She again lies down and slept but this time she only closed her eyes and didn't fall in sleep. Seeing her, AAZARO again fell in his sleep. The bright sunny morning came. With bearing the strange feelings they both began to move towards their kingdom. In the noon they reached and AAZARO escorted MORENA.

MORENA: "this is my house, thank you for dropping me till here; it was a pleasure to accomplish this journey with a great warrior."

AAZARO (bearing a fake smile on his face): "it was pleasure of mine too."

They both shook their hands and moved towards their destinations. AAZARO reached to his palace and was welcomed in royal manners, on the other hand, MORENA entered in her house and she was too welcomed. They both took the blessings of their elders and went to their room. Everything was there with them but something very important was missing." What was that?" they both asked this particular question to themselves. In MORENA's house VAROCIA entered in her room and asked MORENA to sit with her. They both sat and the conversation began.

VAROCIA: "you are fresh now?"

MORENA: "yes, I am fine now."

VAROCIA: "tell me about your journey, I think it must be quite exciting."

MORENA: "yes it was."

VAROCIA: "is everything ok with you dear, I can't find the exact happiness that should be seen on your face now."

MORENA: "I am totally fine but slightly tired, please allow me to fall in sleep in your lap."

VAROCIA: "yes, sweet heart." . . . . MORENA slept in her mother's lap. The evening came and again VAROCIA entered in MORENA's room.

VAROCIA: "why are you not ready dear?"

MORENA: "ready for what?"

VAROCIA: "today, there is a celebration in the palace and you two, AAZARO and you will be awarded with new names, this celebration is only for you both, today is a big day for you.",

MORENA: "mother, you know it well, I didn't decide to go this quest for this new name or award, I did this for you both and for me.",

VAROCIA: "my dear, you are saying as if I don't know the reason but my sweet little daughter, this day is a great day for me and your father, today in front of whole ANALASKA, you will be revered for your achievements and for your hard work, seeing all this in front for a parent is biggest achievement. Don't banish me and your father from this happiness."

MORENA (hold her mother's hand): "mother, seeing you and father happy is more important for me and I will come, but mother I have never been to the palace ever."

VAROCIA: "you have never been to anywhere because you only used to visit your favorite jungle."

MORENA: "mother did I hear the name AAZARO?"

VAROCIA: "yes, dear, he is the prince of ANALASKA and today will be made a king of this kingdom."

MORENA (in shock): "what? He is the prince of ANALASKA?"

VAROCIA: "he didn't tell you about him?"

MORENA: "not at all, he didn't tell me anything about him, he told me that he is a prince but not this, that he is the prince of ANALASKA."

VAROCIA: "must be he met you as a warrior that's why he didn't tell you anything about him."

MORENA: "whatever mother, he should tell me his reality, this is cheating."

Suddenly LORIYA entered in the room.

LORIYA: "MORENAAAAAAAAAAAA! How are you my dear friend?" She hugged MORENA and showed her happiness.

LORIYA: "MADAM VAROCIA, kindly allows me to make my friend ready for the party tonight."

VAROCIA: "Off course, this is the dresses I got for her."

LORIYA: "Such a beautiful backless maroon color dress."

MORENA: "mother, you know it very well, I don't wear such dresses."

VAROCIA: "I know this . . . . but for me please, you will look very beautiful. And listen, I and your father are going now so you both get ready and come, ok!!"

MORENA AND LORIYA TOGETHER: "ok!!!!"

They both got ready and came out of their house and started moving towards the palace.

On the other hand, AAZARO was getting ready when LORD NELISH entered in his room.

LORD NELISH: "it's quite good to see you in condition of a warrior. Today is one of the big days of your life AAZARO, today I am going to give you my post because this is the perfect time, I know for you I am making it very fast . . . . but dear son, when this responsibility came to me at that time I was younger and I didn't had such qualities like you possess."

AAZARO: "Father, its honorable thing for me that you think me as deserving for this responsibility . . . . But why me why not LAVINZO and where the hell is he, didn't he complete the quest?"

LORD NELISH: "you both were born at the same time, but you took birth first and then he was born, so . . . . according to the rules you can only be the king and LAVINZO is in his room, he completed only two tasks and he came back to palace."

AAZARO: "but why? What happened? Did he tell you anything?"

LORD NELISH: "Dear son, when he came back he told me that he wants to meditate because he wanted to increase his mental level and he is not at all interested in the quest. He has closed his room since he returned from the quest, I think he has devoted his this time of life to GOD ARMMANDO, I hope his wish comes true. "LORD NELISH took out the special key of the book and handed it to AAZARO and said, "after the ceremony is over, meet me in the midst of the palace, I will tell you the importance of the key.",

AAZARO: "midst of the palace, where?"

LORD NELISH: "don't bother; ALBERT CRUZ will take you over there." . . . .

After this long conversation they both left the room and went to the hall. Everyone knew that LAVINZO is meditating, but no one knew exactly for what and for whom he was meditating. Only JUDASE knew the answer but he was very quiet. AAZARO and LORD NELISH entered in the hall, the hall was full of people and it was like the whole ANALASKA came to see their new king.

THE CEREMONY OF WARRIORS

EVERYTHING was there in the hall for AAZARO but something was missing but "what was that?", his friends were present, his relatives and even his most loving MADAM VAROCIA was present but he was not able to understand what was missing and then suddenly the missing thing came in his front. He saw MORENA in unbelievable manner. She was wearing a maroon dress and for the first time in his life he saw her open, long, golden, brown wavy hair, she was looking out of the world to him. AAZARO was not able to stop staring at her and then LORD NELISH announced for the ball room dance. One by one every couple of the hall was coming on the dance floor to dance even the queen and king was dancing together. AAZARO didn't think of anything and he moved to ask MORENA for the dance, while he was coming near to her, she noticed him and her eyes stopped staring in shy when he came near to her.

AAZARO: "can I have the pleasure to dance with the beautiful lady." VAROCIA was standing with MORENA and she kept her hand in his hand and said, "Off course my dear". They both went on the dance floor. For the first time in MORENA's life somebody touched her in this manner. It was quite harsh to explain. They both were continuously looking in each other as if; they are only present in the hall. A very different and unimaginable feeling was revolving in the mind of both of them. AAZARO was holding her in such a way that he doesn't want her to go away from him and MORENA was lost in his arms. It was felt that they both wanted the time to be stopped. Their mysterious love was noticed by most of the people but no one uttered a single word.

When JUBEELIA noticed them she came near to VAROCIA and said, "Did she tell you anything about her feelings?"

VAROCIA: "no, not at all, did AAZARO tell anything to you?"

JUBEELIA: "nothing, he told me nothing."

The dance was not looking like a dance; MORENA and AAZARO were lost in their different world. They were lost in themselves, and the time came when they both were about to kiss each other again and suddenly MORENA saw something and she left AAZARO like anything. She moved back and did not turn to his side, AAZARO was quite shocked but he also didn't reveal his feelings to her and then LORD NELISH reached to the stage to make the important announcement.

LORD NELISH: "THE PEOPLE OF ANALASKA, I WANT TO YOU ALL TO HEAR THE IMPORTANT NEWS. TODAY YOU ALL ARE GOING TO HAVE YOUR NEW KING BUT BEFORE THAT, I WANT TO REVEAL THE WARRIORS WHO WON THE QUEST AND CAME BACK SAFELY TO THE KINGDOM. FIRSTLY

I WOULD LIKE TO CALL CAPRION, THE TEACHER AND THE MOST SUITABLE LORD OF ARMY OF OUR KINGDOM. CAPRION PLEASE COME HERE AND TAKE THIS IN YOUR HONOUR." CAPRION came on the stage and LORD NELISH gave him a very different sword and said, "This is the sword of our ancestors and today I give the responsibility of this important sword. This is very important for me to revere you by this thing, only you can be the suitable teacher of my children, who taught them everything that a warrior should learn and because of you only, today I will be able to make my son the king of this kingdom, you made him to stand at this position." LORD NELISH hugged CAPRION and then again talked to the mob again.

"NOW I AM VERY GLAD TO CALL MORENA AND AAZARO, THE WARRIORS OF THE KINGDOM TO COME HERE AND TAKE THE BLESSINGS OF ALL THE PEOPLE AND ACCEPT THE POSITION THAT I AM GOING TO GIVE THEM."

They both walked towards the stage and LORD NELISH firstly talked to MORENA and said, "From the day my son has arrived from the journey he only talks about you and your decisions, he told me everything about you, even about your first meeting with him. I am not at all angry on you . . . . don't you dare to think of it but I am impressed by your deeds and your opinions; today I want you to take the position of an advisor in this palace". Before MORENA speaks anything, LORD NELISH stopped her by saying that, "MORENA, my child I am not only giving you this responsibility because of your quality of a warrior but I am giving you this responsibility because I think you are the only and exact owner of this position. Please don't say no, it's my request." When MORENA heard these words she was speechless and in order to respect a king's request, she agreed. Then again, LORD NELISH came back to AAZARO and conducted his mob, "MY ALL THE LOVING PEOPLE OF THE KINGDOM . . . . I WANT YOU ALL TO WELCOME AND HONOUR THE NEW KING OF THE KINGDOM, THE SON OF NELISH, AAZARO." Before this the whole ANALASKA was clapping but this time the sound was not at all stopping.

LORD NELISH: "HE IS THE ONLY ONE WHO STANDS FOR THIS POSITION; MANY PEOPLE WENT TO THE AREA OF OUR JUNGLE.... BUT NO ONE WAS ABLE TO GET THOSE RELIEVE FROM KREYEAT.... BUT MY SON DID THIS, HE MADE ALL THE PEOPLETO BE FEARLESS, HE ABLOISHED THEIR FEAR AND MADE FREE EVERYONE AND GOT THIS SWORD.... WHICH IS MY FATHER'S SWORD." LORD NELISH turned to AAZARO and said this is very sacred sword my son, this is your grandfather's sword, LORD CEREAL's sword, it was stolen from me somehow but you again got this to me, you know except the person who is pious, courageous and unbiased purely.... no one else in this world can hold this sword and you possess all such quality in yourself. "TODAY, I AM VERY GLAD TO ANNOUNCE THAT AAZARO IS THE KING OF THIS KINGDOM." While the king was speaking these words, AAZARO interrupted him and said, "I AM NOT THE ONLY OWNER OF THIS PRAISE BUT SOMEONE ELSE IS ALSO THEIR IN THIS HALL.... WHO NEEDS AND DESERVE THIS APPERICIATION ALONG WITH ME. WHEN I WENT NEAR TO THE SWORD, I TRIED TO TAKE IT OUT FROM THE EYES OF KREYEATH BUT I WAS UNABLE TO DO SO AND THEN NOTICED THAT SOMEONE ELSE ALSO HELPING ME TO TAKE IT OUT AND THAT PERSON WAS MISS MORENA." He pointed his hand towards MORENA and everybody stared at her and she felt embarrassing. Again he said, "CAN I HAVE YOU HERE MISS MORENA?" LORIYA standing just beside her pushed her to go on stage again. LORIYA said, "Come on MORENA just go, go, and go. MORENA went to the stag and AAZARO hold her hands and turned towards the mob and said," AS THE KING TOLD YOU ALL THE SWORD REQUIRED PIOUNESS, COURAGEOUS FEELINGS AND UNBIASSNESS, I THINK I DON'T POSSESS ALL THESE QUALITY FULLY. He turned towards MORENA and said," I THINK MISS MORENA COMPLETED MYSELF AND BECAUSE OF HER ONLY I TOOK OUT THAT SWORD FROM THEIR. SHE DIDN'T ONLY HEPLED BUT FOR ME SHE GOT HURT AND INJURED, IN ORDER TO SAVE MY LIFE. WE BOTH HAD COMPLETED OUR TASK EARLIER BUT WE CAME LATE BECAUSE SHE WAS INJURED, SHE WAS FIGHTING FOR HER LIFE, SHE WAS FIGHTING FOR HER BREATHS BECAUSE....

IF SHE WOULDN'T HAVE BEEN THEIR THIS TIME YOU ALL MUST NOT BE MEETING YOUR NEW KING. NOT ONLY AS AN ADVISOR BUT ALL THESE QUALITIES IN A LADY OF OUR KINGDOM SHOULD MAKES US ALL TO FELL PROUD ON OURSELVES. I WANT YOU ALL TO CLAP FOR HER SO LOUDLY SO THAT EACH AND EVERY PARTICLE SHOULD LISTEN THESE CLAPPING AND REVERE HER." After the words of AAZARO, the people of ANALASKA honored her by huge round of applause. CAPRION and VAROCIA felt proud on their daughter and LORD NELISH asked MORENA to give that sword to AAZARO by her. After she handled him the sword, AAZARO was took near to the royal throne and LORD NELISH made him to sit and then JUBEELIA made him to wear the golden crown. The crown of the king had a symbol of rising sun just same as the flag of the kingdom in which rising sun was there on the back of a lion. At that time, AAZARO was asked to take the oath. ALBERT CRUZ was speaking the oath and AAZARO was repeating his words. In a great manner, AAZARO became the king of the kingdom. Everyone in the kingdom was very happy from its new king but someone was there in the ceremony who didn't like this decision at all, that was JUDASE. While AAZARO was repeating his oath JUDASE hurled his drink and walked away from their and move towards the room of LAVINZO. He just pushed the door violently and shouted on LAVINZO.

JUDASE: "You fool, what the hell are you doing here and what do you think, by doing such things you can be the king of the kingdom?" LAVINZO didn't respond on the words of him he was very quiet just like a silent ocean.

JUDASE: "LAVINZO!!!!!, I got you as my product of my worships, I thought LORD HEAZER is very glad by seeing my devotion towards him . . . . but I think it was my biggest mistake to ask you from him, you are useless for me, you can't do anything, you are a coward; I thought you will help me for spreading the evil power in this kingdom but I was so wrong." In anger JUDASE hurled a vase towards him and before that vas hurt LAVINZO, he opened his eyes and that has turned into ashes. He stood up from the mat at which he was sitting and meditating, he took up upper clothes and wore it. He gave a very devious smile on his face and walked towards JUDASE, he held his both hands and suddenly the hands of JUDASE started turning blue, he felt as if his hands has become numb and after that his hands started turning red and again he felt that he has kept his hands in an oven. JUDASE moved back and pulled his hands from LAVINZO.

LAVINZO: "now also do you think I am useless? What did you think of me, am I joke or something else? You said that you got me as the product of your worships and because of your immense devotion towards your god HEAZER?"

JUDASE: "yes!!!!"

LAVINZO (IN MORE LOUDER WAY): "then how you can have doubt on his powers, you imbecile. Do you really want to know that why did I leave the quest and started meditating?"

JUDASE (IN PUZZLING AND WHOOPING MANNER): "yes, I do want to know.

LAVINZO (AGAIN IN SMILING): "actually, I am the product of your immense devotion; I am here to spread evil empire in not only this kingdom but in the every corner of this EARTH. The quest was for the warriors and I gassed that I am not a warrior, I am an evil whose powers are now immense, who can own any power, who is able to spread the evils everywhere now. The exact time has come!!!"

JUDASE: "how can you decide the exact time?"

LAVINZO: "this is the only difference between you and me, you are here in this kingdom for long time but till yet . . . . you were not able to do everything. But don't worry now . . . . I will tell you what you have to do."

JUDASE: "I have done nothing? What do you mean?"

LAVINZO: "what do you think JUDASE, killing your parents at very early age is the biggest task or killing my grandfather LORD DION was the biggest achievement for you?"

JUDASE got a huge shock because except him no one knew about his all these deeds.

LAVINZO: "don't worry!!!! Me belong to you and tonight is the full moon night. Yes?"

JUDASE: "yes!!!"

LAVINZO: "we need to move towards PIERO where the dead bodies of all these people are lying."

JUDASE: "how do you know that I buried their dead bodies in PIERO?"

LAVINZO: "we don't have enough time to waste, before this full moon gets covered by the clouds . . . . We have to reach there."

JUDASE: "whatever you say my lord!!!"

LAVINZO: "and there is one work for you."

JUDASE: "what?"

LAVINZO whispered something in JUDASE ears and they both moved in different directions. While walking towards his door, LAVINZO noticed a girl coming near to his room. He had the first glance over her face and got lost seeing her beauty. Then he noticed she was coming near to him and that girl was LORIYA.

LORIYA: "are you LAVINZO?"

LAVINZO: "Yes!!!"

LORIYA: "OH! This is great, MADAM JUBEELIA sent me over here to see whether you are done with your work or not."

LAVINZO: "go and tell mother, that my work is over and I am going out for some work and will return very soon."

LAVINZO moved and suddenly LORIYA hold his hands.

LORIYA: "AH! I am sorry but can I ask you where you are going this time, I mean ceremony is here and all the people have gathered here to meet you."

LAVINZO: "don't worry! I will come back very soon."

He left her over there and moved towards PIERO. LAVINZO felt something for a girl in his life for the first time. Ignoring her, LAVINZO moved for his vicious work. LORIYA informed JUBEELIA about LAVINZO. When LORD NELISH was talking to ALBERT CRUZ, JUDASE came near to him and whispered something in his ears and NELISH said that I am coming in fraction of seconds. LORD NELISH called ALBERT CRUZ to get AAZARO in the secret room as soon as possible. ALBERT CRUZ took AAZARO in the secret where the book "two face coin" was kept.

AAZARO: "Why you have taken me here?" AAZARO saw LORD NELISH standing in front of him. He held his hand and took him near to the book.

LORD NELISH: "AAZARO, this is the secret room of ANALASKA where this sacred book is kept."

AAZARO: "sacred book? Why this book is here and why you kept it so safely?"

LORD NELISH: "My dear son!!!!!!!!! Listen to me very carefully, whatever I am going to tell you. At the early time . . . . when this EARTH was made by GOD ARMMANDO AND GOD HEAZER then they divided it into five kingdoms. All these kingdoms where handled to five kings who have been seen the most powerful and wise. They all completed the quest as you did. After such hard work, Gods saw the quality of a warrior as well as the savior in them and they were then made a king. Many generations passed away and the sons of every king started ruling the kingdom after they completed the quest. These qualities of warrior and savior began to flow in hierarchy. The five kingdoms are like five fingers of hand, when you close it, it becomes the power and when you open it, and it becomes the weakness. ANALASKA; THE BRIZON KINGDOM RULED BY LORD BRIZON; THE THRIYON KINGDOM RULED BY LORD THRIYON; THE DION'S KINGDOM RULED BY YOUR GRAND FATHER LORD DION AND THE LAST THE ZUERO'S KINGDOM RULED BY LORD ZUERO. These are the five kingdoms and the kings. In these five kingdoms their lives ten people. Every kingdom has two messengers of God . . . . like LADY DUNNA and IRISH in our kingdom. The 10 people possess very different powers in them and these kingdoms are highly powerful because of such people. The most powerful kingdom in all of them is our kingdom because this is the only kingdom where each and every problems and dilemmas are solved by this book, this is the place where you can find every answer and every secret lying in heart of this kingdom and the most important thing and the most powerful reason is that whenever any king, queen or any savior man or woman dies then their spirits don't go to hell or heaven but they resides in the middle of the palace in other secret room. The savior spirits always saves this kingdom from every evil power and that's why we have two graveyards, the graveyard of prisoners is different. Today I am telling you these things because these all things are very important that should be known by the king."

AAZARO: "Father!!! This is the very big responsibility you are giving me."

LORD NELISH: "You are the king now and as a king you have to take all these big responsibility on your shoulders. My son, this sword is the fifth sword given by ARMMANDO to the five kings; this sword can abolish any powerful evil power man or woman. It's not mere to understand everything but listen, humans are very weak, and they all possess avarice, bad thoughts and many weakness. This weakness turns them into evil. Till the human do not overcome their weakness, the evils will be residing in the kingdoms. Big responsibility, big powers and more vicious danger. Humans can be evils but evils can't be humans.

AAZARO: "What are you talking about father? What you mean by evils and humans?" LORD NELISH took out the key of the book and handled it to him and said, "I told it's not so mere to understand everything, experience is a good teacher, you will learn everything."

AAZARO: "What is this father?"

LORD NELISH: "This is the key of this book; the book can't be opened without this."

AAZARO: "CAN YOU SHOW ME?"

LORD NELISH: "Now I am no more a king so I can't open this, it can only be opened by the queen or the king of the kingdom and now you are the king."

KING AAZARO sees the key . . . . it seemed like a very small box of metal in silver color. The small box like key had a small red color point in the middle, very different signs were made on the key, some very different flowers and some thorns were only understandable.

ALBERT CRUZ: "KING AAZARO just presses the red point and the key will open."

AAZARO pressed the red point and the key suddenly got opened, the triangle shaped petal opened. There were only five petals. AAZARO inserted the key in the book lock and turned it. The book opened!!!!!

AAZARO: "Blank pages? . . . . Father!!! . . . . nothing is written here."

ALBERT CRUZ: "the book is always blank . . . . it writes only then, when you asked any question or solution for any unsolved any questions."

AAZARO: "I want to ask something? I want to know who will be the queen and most loyal person of the kingdom." After the question was made . . . . the book wrote something.

AAZARO: "What is written over here, I can't read it?"

ALBERT CRUZ: "No one can do so except me because this responsibility is on my shoulders."

AAZARO: "And if you are not here, then?"

ALBERT CRUZ: "Then a person who will possess my qualities in him will be able to read it and don't worry my king . . . . That person will come by himself in front of you after me."

δύναμημισό σας θα είναι η βασίλισσα του βασιλείου και το πιο πιστό άτομοτου βασιλείου σας και θα σας το πρόσωπο στο οποίο η πίστηρέειστο αίμα.

After ALBERT CRUZ spelled the words, the two doors behind the book turned into faces and the first face spoke, "your destiny is quite crucial on your life, a time will come when you have to choose between your love and your responsibility." and the other face spoke, "don't go after your destiny, and just have the zest of your life."

AAZARO: "I remember my first task to take the right path."

ALBERT CRUZ: "Whatever you have learned by your quest you have to use all those thoughts in your life as a king." AAZARO looked at the sword and key again and afterwards they all moved back to hall. LORD NELISH remembered that JUDASE called him and he said

AAZARO that he is coming within few seconds. LORD NELISH came out of the palace and saw JUDASE standing near the gate.

JUDASE: "hurry brother, hurry. They both walked forth but NELISH what the big cat JUDASE was having in his mind."

NELISH: "JUDASE, I gas that we are proceeding towards PIERO."

JUDASE: "Yes brother, I want to show you something." They both entered in the graveyard.

NELISH: "What do you want to show me here?", while speaking these words lord NELISH noticed the dead body LORD DION and a hypnotized LADY DUNNA.

LORD NELISH: "LORD DION, he is dead and what has happened to LADY DUNNA." He went near to LADY DUNNA AND SAID, "LADY DUNNA, what's wrong with you? LADY DUNNA! Speak up!!!!!!" LADY DUNNA looked upon LORD NELSIH and her eyes were pure black; LORD NELISH moved back and JUDASE held him.

LORD NELISH: "Did you do this JUDASE? (He held his collars) how dare you? I thought you are my brother, why all these graves are open? What kind of black magic you are doing here?" When LORD NELISH was speaking these words someone backstabbed him, he turned and saw it was LAVINZO. He held him and said, "LAVINZO you too are a . . . ."

LAVINZO: "Yes, father I am also an evil, a pure evil."

While holding him LORD NELISH died. LAVINZO left his body and ask JUDASE to keep the dead body on the grave near to LORD DION'S grave. LORD DION, LORD NELISH and LADY DUNNA they three were lying respectively. LAVINZO set down their heads, closed his eyes and started his rituals. He was wearing black attire. When the moon came out of the dark clouds then he opened his eyes, which appeared jet black. He kept his swords on their head and suddenly a great thunder came on it. The shinning thunders were directly going onto LAVINZO'S body. He was shouting like anything. The thunders were not only coming from the clouds but from the moon too. After few minutes, it stopped the spirits of two of them one of LORD NELISH and other of LADY DUNNA went to its right place but the spirit of LORD DION went inside LAVINZO. After this when he opened his eyes, his eyes were of two colors i.e. red and black.

JUDASE: "What you done my lord?"

LAVINZO (showing evil smile): "now I possess all the powers of the two lords and LADY DUNNA."

JUDASE: "But the spirits of LORD NELISH and LADY DUNNA has gone and you only have LORD DION's soul in you."

LAVINZO: "Again remember my words JUDASE, I said I possess the powers of them . . . . not the souls, I know that I have only one soul i.e. LORD DION's. But whatever I needed . . . . I got it. I don't require any soul, but a time will come when I will make this impossible thing possible."

JUDASE: "What will you do with these dead bodies?"

LAVINZO: "What is done with the dead bodies?"

JUDASE understood the words of LAVINZO and once again he did what he did with the body of LORD DION. The party got over and all the people went back to their houses. AAZARO being the king came out of the palace to escort MORENA. While they both were talking AAZARO saw LAVINZO and JUDASE coming from outside. Seeing LAVINZO back, AAZARO hugged him. AAZARO SAID, "I am happy brother, you came back; are you finish with your meditational work?, just leave it and meet MORENA, the new advisor of our kingdom and LORIYA the most beautiful girl and MORENA, LORIYA this is my fraternal brother LAVINZO." MORENA and LORIYA talked to him and then they both left and moved for their houses.

VIRONOCCE

AAZARO and LAVINZO were talking to each other in gallery of the palace when they heard their mother's loud voice. They both entered in her room.

AAZARO: "What happen to you mother why are you shouting?"

JUBEELIA: "When did you see your father last?"

AAZARO: "I met him just half an hour ago, why?"

JUBEELIA: "Do you know that where your father is?"

AAZARO: "He must be somewhere in palace."

JUBEELIA: "I have seen each and every room of palace, at least three times."

The tension rises and AAZARO called his guards. The guards entered in the room. AAZARO: "Just see where my father is? Some of you search in the palace and some go to the kingdom and see where he has gone." Without knowing any reason, JUBEELIA don't know why was looking LAVINZO with accusing eyes. Even LAVINZO was not able to see in the eyes of his mother, he knew that what he has done.

AAZARO: "I am also going in the kingdom to search for him."

LAVINZO moved to his room and left JUBEELIA to remember the words of ARMMANDO once again. The whole night AAZARO was searching for his father but didn't get any news of him. In the next morning after getting the news, each and everybody related to the palace started searching for him but no one got him. While searching for LORD NELISH, MORENA saw the band of his hand which had the sign of ANALASKA, a golden band having rising sun on it. She remembered that she saw this band in his hand last night. She found the band just near to PIERO. She was about to go in . . . . but an old man who was the guard there, stopped her and said, "I am sorry my daughter . . . . but no one is allowed to go in this graveyard."

MORENA: "I am sorry! But why I can't go inside?"

OLD MAN: "Because, this is the graveyard of prisoners, the bad people . . . . their souls directly go to hell and my lord, my king has ordered me to do so, I am sorry!!!! This area is prohibited."

MORENA: "It's ok, thank you!!!!!!"

She didn't go inside but she had the feelings that something wrong was there and what was that?, she did not know. She and all the people who went on search came back to palace, they all didn't get any news of him but when MORENA came back and showed what she got from PIERO, JUBEELIA just took that band from her and said, "there is no need now to search for him, I know where he has gone. So, gentleman and the king please get back to your work there is lot more to do."

AAZARO: "But, mother we can't give up, hardly matters we didn't get news until now; it must be that he has gone to some other kingdom.",

JUBEELIA (having click smile on her face): "AAZARO, just do as I said.",

AAZARO was about to argue but MORENA held his hands and he didn't speak. JUBEELIA keeping the band in her hands went in her room. The whole ANALASKA went in sorrow but it was quite surprising to know that JUBEELIA didn't cry and on that night only, another surprising thing happened. JUDASE called all the important members of the palace and JUBEELIA and said, "Before being escaped, my elder brother told me his last wish. I want to tell you all that what his last wish was."

AAZARO: "Please, tell me what that is?"

JUDASE: "He wanted to divide the kingdom. So that both the brothers can hold their rights and shouldn't bear the feeling of jealousy."

AAZARO: "Jealousy? Why we both will be having this feeling?"

JUDASE: "The feelings are not made by us but they make their place by itself." JUBEELIA: "I need one day time to consider this."

AAZARO: "Mother, what is the need of considering this? If this was the only last wish of my father then we should respect this and do it."

JUBEELIA: "My lord, please allow me?"

AAZARO: "Mother, don't make me feel abased."

JUBEELIA left the hall after listening AAZARO and everybody around also went to their work. That night was very crucial for everyone but mostly for JUBEELIA, she was quiet and she was not saying anything. It was like a volcano erupting in her heart. The next morning came and all the people gathered in the hall, AAZARO, LAVINZO, JUDASE, MORENA and others were waiting for the decision.

JUBEELIA: "I know for what you all are waiting, but firstly I want to tell you something i.e. LORD NELISH is dead, he is no more and my father LORD DION is also dead." A shocking wave abolished the thoughts of everyone in the hall except LAVINZO and JUDASE. Everyone became speechless.

JUBEELIA: "I know what are you thinking now and how I know this, it's not important that how I know this but this is important that what we have to do now. There will be the partition of ANALASKA. THIS KINGDOM WILL BE DIVIDED IN TWO EQUAL PARTS BETWEEN MY BOTH SONS. A COURT WILL BE FORMED FOR THESE BOTH KINGDOMS SO THAT INJUSTICE AND LOSS OF HARMONY SHOULDN'T BE PART BETWEEN THESE

KINGDOMS. THIS PART WHERE WE ALL ARE STANDING . . . . WILL BE OF AAZARO'S AND THE PART FROM WHERE THE JUNGLE ENDS THAT WILL BE THE PART OF LAVINZO. THE COURT WHICH WILL FORM WOULD BE HAVING THREE PEOPLE, THE SON OF GOD ARMMANDO 'ALEC', THE SON OF GOD HEAZER 'DEFRON' AND LAST THE HEAD OF THE COURT 'VIRONOCCE'. HE IS NOT THE SON OF ANYONE BUT ONCE WHEN THE POWERS OF ARMMANDO AND HEAZER CAME OUT OF THEM WHEN THEY WERE MEDITATING THEN HE TOOK BIRTH. THE NAME OF THE COURT WILL BE 'TYMONE'. THIS COURT WILL BE LOCATED IN BETWEEN BOTH OF THE KINGDOMS. IN ORDER TO BALANCE THE PEACE BETWEEN BOTH THE KINGDOMS, I HAVE TAKEN THIS DECISION. ANY DECISION REGARDING BOTH THE KINGDOMS WILL BE TAKEN BY THEM."

LAVINZO: "When they will be taking all the decisions regarding our kingdoms then they should be made the kings, what is our need?"

JUBEELIA: "I didn't mean that, I want to tell you one thing that regarding both the kingdoms they will be taking decisions means they will only take decisions when both the kingdoms are involved, whatever you both do in your kingdoms that none of their business."

AAZARO: "Mother, whatever you want will be done!!!!"

JUBEELIA: "One thing more, LORD NELISH has given the key of the book to AAZARO so I can't do anything related to this book, the book can't be displaced and I can't take the key from him. So, the book will be here only. AAZARO, LAVINZO I want to talk to both of you in night."

So, move for you works and meet me in my room at night. With these perturbing words she left the hall. MORENA was quietly looking at the face of AAZARO, he had only pain but being the king he was not able to show that to anyone. After the decision was listened, they started moving for their work. LAVINZO and JUDASE moved for their new palace. AAZARO left the hall and moved to his room and MORENA followed him. She entered in his room and saw him standing in the balcony. MORENA felt that he was in such a pain to which he was not able to explain it to anyone. She went near to him and kept her hand on his shoulder and said, "AAZARO (He turned to her), I know you are not at all happy with the decisions, I know this too that you will never ever forget your brother or your father, this time I want to talk to AAZARO a mere AAZARO not the king of the kingdom, can you allow me?"

AAZARO: "Yes, off course!!!!"

MORENA: "AAZARO, don't feel bad she is your mother and if she has taken such decision then, there must be some reason. This is very crucial time and I want say, ah!!, I just want to say . . . . she hugged him very tightly, I want to say I am always with you; never ever think that you are alone. I will always be there for you." AAZARO too needed her company and he also held her and said, "How do you know that I was feeling alone?"

MORENA: "I just saw your feelings in your eyes. "She wanted to leave him but he was not allowing her to go. Then ALBERT CRUZ knocked on the door. They both left each other.

ALBERT CRUZ: "LAVINZO is leaving this kingdom now. So your mother wants to meet both of you."

AAZARO: "I am coming." ALBERT CRUZ left the room after listening the answer.

AAZARO: "Thank you, for understanding my feelings." MORENA smiled and AAZARO moved to his mother's room. In JUBEELIA'S room LAVINZO was already present. JUBEELIA was standing near her wedding's painting, when AAZARO entered in the room she turned towards both of them.

JUBEELIA: "When I was a young girl, I met a man in my life for whom I felt something, to make him to come in my life I prayed to GOD ARMMANDO so much, so that I can spend my whole life with him and see my wish came true but there was something else too that I got from him. He gave me some supernatural powers and said, a time will come in my life when I would have to give these powers to someone who can give ANALASKA a bright future. Your father is not here and without him there is no meaning of living, I think ARMMANDO must have pointed this time, I don't know whether I have taken a right decision or not but I can't differentiate between my own blood, today I am going to distribute this power between you both and hope that you will utilize it for the welfare of this kingdom." JUBEELIA just closed her eyes and moved her hands around her heart and a very special kind of energy came out, she divided the energy and kept it on her both hands, her both hands delivered the powers to both the kings, the room was sparkling and it was the last time of JUBEELIA, after the powers were distributed JUBEELIA fell down on the floor and AAZARO, LAVINZO they both held her.

JUBEELIA: "AAZARO, LAVINZO my children, I don't know whether I was bias or unbiased with both of you, but I know this that I loved my both the children a lot, your father too loved you both very much and when he is not here then there is no meaning for me to stay alive, I am going near to him, my children please do me a last favor, just bury my dead body in PIERO, I think I have done a crime and I should be punished for that. Please children complete my wish."

The shaking and whooping voice of JUBEELIA stopped and she died. AAZARO and LAVINZO both had tears in their eyes; AAZARO kept her mother's body on the bed and called the guards to call all the men of palace. In the evening all of them gathered and her body was buried in PIERO. AAZARO didn't show his tears to anyone and not even LAVINZO showed any kind of sadness. After the ceremony was done LAVINZO hugged his brother and moved towards his new palace, that evening AAZARO didn't eat anything he was just alone and very quiet. In the evening, when MORENA had to leave for her home, she went in the room of AAZARO to tell him the important thing. She entered in his room.

MORENA: "AAZARO, tomorrow we both have to go to the partition place, where the jungle ends and LAVINZO'S KINGDOMS begins.

We need to reach their in the morning so that we can meet the judges of TYMONE's court."

AAZARO didn't reply to her and she wished him good night and came out of the room. MORENA was very confused because she has never ever seen such behavior of AAZARO. She came back to her house.

VAROCIA: "Dear, just change your clothes and come on the table for dinner."

MORENA: "Mother, just not willing to eat anything."

VAROCIA: "Why my dear, are you ok? Tell me what's wrong . . . . any problem?"

MORENA: "Mother, I am fine, but only little bit tired, want to take rest."

VAROCIA: "Ok, my child."

VAROCIA kissed the forehead of MORENA and then MORENA leaves for her room. She took bath and went on her bed, twisting and turning but not sleeping. She began to talk to herself. MORENA (TALKING TO HERSELF) said, "What is happening to me, why am I feeling painful? It's like AAZARO is in great pain and he is not revealing it to anyone. His calmness is the biggest sign of his pain. What I should do, I can't see him like this, I don't know why, but I can't see him in more pain." While she was talking to herself AAZARO was also wide awake but he was not crying, he was numb, it was like he has lost his happiness and his smile somewhere. When both pious souls were having such feelings at that time, the evil power reached to its destination. LAVINZO reached to a very calm and quiet place, there was a very big volcano and inside the volcano LAVINZO formed his palace, it was the area where the greenery of jungle ends and the darkness begins, the place was very suspicious and it was all dark everywhere. JUDASE and LAVINZO entered in their new palace, the hot lava was visible, the palace looked as if, it is the most evil place of the world. From inside it was much bigger than the palace of AAZARO but the brightness of purity was absent. JUDASE by his powers called all the evil spirits from DION'S kingdom, the evils had already turned the people of DION'S kingdom evil. After JUDASE performed rituals to call the evil spirits, he moved to the hall where LAVINZO was sitting on his throne.

JUDASE: "My patience has given fruitful results to me. Today is the happiest day of my life because I am able to see you as a king; my lord, I want to ask something, can I?"

LAVINZO: "Off course!!!"

JUDASE: "Why did JUBEELIA called you in the room and what she did that she lost her life?"

LAVINZO: "My mother, poor mother, she called me in the room to increase my powers."

JUDASE: "Your powers, how she can increase your powers? She was a mere woman and she was not an evil also."

LAVINZO: "You're mistaken my dear, you think that only evils can increase the powers of an evil?"

JUDASE: "Yes!!!!"

LAVINZO: "PITY, poor guy you don't know that the weaknesses of humans only, increase our powers." LAVINZO came near to JUDASE and said, "Evil always dominates the goodness very vastly but goodness and piousness always takes a lot of time to reach at the apex of evils. Be very clear JUDASE, we only rule because of the weaknesses of humans and by dominating on their goodness, humans will always be having their weaknesses. So, we will always going rule here. JUDASE AND LAVINZO had a big laugh and they began with their chapter of life. On the other hand, the whole ANALASKA was wrapped in the blanket of sorrow. AAZARO, who lost everything in his life, was under a lot of pressure and tension, the pain became his part of life; he was not able to see anything neither any parent nor any friend. MORENA was also under miserable feelings, she was quite unhappy with the pathetic condition of AAZARO, she did not understand that she has fallen in love with him, and AAZARO had the essence of this but now he was trying to escape from her. Now AAZARO got the feelings of being hapless for everyone and he doesn't want to be the reason of black clouds on MORENA'S life. That night was the night to take the right decision for everyone. AAZARO took a very crucial and vicious decision for his life that he will never get close to MORENA. The new morning came with a new AAZARO, who really wants to rule his own kingdom with full his devotion. MORENA, ALBERT CRUZ and CAPRION came to the hall where AAZARO was sitting on the throne and waiting for them.

AAZARO: "I think we all should move for the court." MORENA was about to say something but she felt that AAZARO is trying to avoid her and she didn't speak. They all proceeded towards the court; they all reached at end of the jungle from where the kingdom of LAVINZO began. LAVINZO and JUDASE were waiting for them and AAZARO with his fellows arrived.

ALBERT CRUZ: "We all are here for formation of new court, the TYMONE court, we all need to close our eyes and call our gods to come here and make this happen." All the people closed their eyes and called their gods. By the prayers, GOD ARMMANDO and GOD HEAZER came at that place.

ARMMANDO: "I know for what you all have called us." GOD ARMMANDO AND GOD HEAZER, they used their powers and made a very big and vast court and named it TYMONE court. GOD ARMMANDO called his son ALEC and GOD HEAZER called his son DEFRONE and then VIRONOCCE was called. VIRONOCCE was the very different personality in amongst all of them, he was wearing a heavy black color coat with red collar inside, he had white golden hair and he had potion on his head in which roaring lion was made. ALEC the son of ARMMANDO was wearing a white color dress and DEFRONE was wearing a dark brown dress. They all had their very different personality but VIRONOCCE was quite different in them.

GOD ARMMANDO: "From AAZARO'S side my son will be appointed, if he will have any problem my son ALEC will tell or convey the message to VIRONOCCE to take the right decision."

GOD HEAZER: "From LAVINZO'S side, my son DEFRONE will be appointed and he will convey his messages."

GOD ARMMANDO (pointing all the people): "I hope, there will not be any loss of harmony and peace will always reside in your kingdoms." With these words the Gods disappeared. The rest of the people entered in the court, there was a big throne and at the both sides two small thrones were kept. VIRONOCCE sat on the big throne and then ALEC and DEFRONE sat respectively.

VIRONOCCE: "I want to tell you all that I am the head of the court but I will not be partial to anyone, so be very clear that I will always take the right decision."

AAZARO: "We hope so!!!!"

LAVINZO: "We know so!!!!" All of them after meeting with the judges went back to their kingdom. AAZARO and MORENA reached at their kingdom but quietness was along with them, whenever she was trying to talk . . . . he was just avoiding her and trying to stay away from her. This behavior of AAZARO was troubling MORENA, she was not understanding why he was doing so. This behavior of AAZARO persisted and two weeks passed away and MORENA by this separation, got closer to AAZARO. One day when she came to the palace in the morning, she found AAZARO not being present in the palace and no one had any information of him. She went to ALBERT CRUZ room. She entered in his room and asked him, "MR. ALBERT CRUZ, do you know where AAZARO is?, I mean where he has gone?," He didn't inform anyone about his secret journey.

ALBERT CRUZ: "You are forgetting one thing MORENA."

MORENA: "He is the king of the kingdom; he doesn't need to inform anyone. I know this very well but as a king he has certain responsibilities and he can't escape form it."

ALBERT CRUZ: "If you really see him as a king then firstly try to see him as a human, as a young boy who lost everything in his life on that very day when he was announced to be the king of the kingdom. He lost his father, his mother and separation from his own real brother, can you feel his pain as a human MISS. MORENA. You were being appointed as an advisor here, what kind of advice you would like to give to your own king, who is smiling in front of all of you with a crying and groaning heart.",

MORENA: "I am sorry MR. ALBERT CRUZ, I never thought of this, I thought with the passage of time he will come out from his pain and heal."

ALBERT CRUZ: "How you can say so. Everyone has something in life or a person in his life with whom or support of them a person can come out of his pain but I can't see anyone being so close to him who can support him or can take him out of this pathetic maze." AEYRENA enters in the room.

AEYRENA: "Good morning MORENA."

MORENA: "Good morning MISS AEYRENA!!!!"

AEYRENA: "You must be getting lot of work every day."

MORENA: "No, nothing is like that." AEYRENA started talking to ALBERT CRUZ and MORENA left the room. MORENA (TALKING TO HERSELF) murmured, "How foolish I am. I didn't think of him at all, MR. ALBERT was right, he lost everything in his life then also he is pretending to be happy in front of everyone but why he is avoiding me, he never did that to me." MORENA was quite tensed and she went to jungle, exactly at that place where she first time kissed AAZARO. She was walking in tension and thinking the methods to take him out of his pain and suddenly she heard something, it was the tunes of a flute that AAZARO played in the quest. She followed the tune and went near that tree where they took rest at once. She saw him playing the flute. She quietly went near to him but having the quality of a warrior, he heard the sound of the quite foots of her and he took out his sword and pointed it towards her.

MORENA: "AAZARO, I am MORENA."

AAZARO: "What are you doing here?"

MORENA: "The same question goes to you."

AAZARO: "I don't think that I need to give any explanation to the advisor of the kingdom, you are the advisor not VIRONOCCE."

MORENA: "I was searching you and when I didn't get the king in the palace so I came here where I used to visit mostly."

AAZARO: "The time has changed MISS MORENA, you are not the mere girl any more, now you are the advisor of the kingdom and I think you must be having a lot of work rather than searching me, I am not an infant."

MORENA: "I know I am not a mere girl any more, but a king has enough work than an advisor." Seeing the negative attitude of AAZARO towards herself she left the place in anger and came back to the kingdom, she didn't go back to the palace on that day. The next morning came with a new shining bright morning but MORENA was not at all about going to the palace, she was not willing to go their but due to her responsibility she went there. AAZARO was waiting for her in the hall and reached at her time.

AAZARO: "On time, good."

MORENA: "Yes, on time!!!!"

AAZARO: "MISS MORENA, I need your help in a case."

MORENA: "Yes, my lord, please tell me, in what manner I can help you."

AAZARO (in a shock by listening the lord from MORENA): "I have to visit ZUERO'S kingdom because LORD ZUERO wants to talk to me about something."

MORENA: "So, what help you need from me?"

AAZARO: "I NEED YOU TO TAKE CARE OF THIS KINGDOM UNTILL, I COME BACK.",

MORENA: "I think more experienced people are there in this palace, you should take help from them."

AAZARO: "I think, I am the king here and your work is to give advice."

MORENA: "Yes my work is to give advice that I have given just now."

AAZARO: "And I listened it, but not willing to follow, and when I don't follow your advice then it's your work to follow my instructions."

MORENA: "Yes, my lord."

AAZARO: "Better!!!!!! I am leaving today and you have to take care of this kingdom, and you don't need to go back to your home you can stay here."

MORENA: "Yes, my lord." After telling the instructions AAZARO left the palace and proceeded for the ZUERO'S KINGDOM. MORENA went to his room and staring at him from the balcony, she was quiet and calm seeing the table turning behavior of AAZARO. She asked one of the guards to inform his parents about her. She started taking care of the kingdom very carefully. One week passed away but AAZARO didn't returned back and again MORENA'S tension raised, she didn't have any idea about him, she wrote a letter and asked a guard to take this letter to AAZARO and asked him where is he, the guard followed her instruction and went to the ZUERO'S kingdom. Again two days passed away but no news came, she was much tensed but why she was in such tension she did not know and the next morning came, in the noon when no news came . . . . MORENA again went to the jungle but this time she was following the other path. She was not aware that where she was going but she was not stopping, she was just following the paths and walking without any destination. While walking she entered in the area where it was like a maze, she heard the sound of roaring, it was not the mere sound but the voice a lion who was roaring but in some other manner. It was like he was groaning in pain. MORENA followed the path where she found a lion caught in trap and the trap was made by a vicious evil. In order to save that lion she took out her sword and began to fight with that evil. She remembered that the swords of these evils are highly poisonous; she took all the steps that she learned and was successful in killing that evil. After killing him, she went near to the lion and opened the chain. She saw that lion was hurt; she took out the piece of cloth from her dress and tied it on his hands. MORENA saw that the lion was afraid of her too, she smiled and said, "Don't worry, I am not going to hurt you, you are fine now and you can move back to the jungle." The lion replied, "I don't live in the jungle." MORENA turned to him in shock. MORENA asked, "You can speak?" The lion again replied, "My name is LEO and I live in ANALASKA."

MORENA: "How you can live in the kingdom? You are an animal." LEO turned to human, a very handsome man.

MORENA: "Oh my god, you are a human, no, you are a lion, who are you?"

LEO: "Don't worry, I am human but I have quality that I can change in form of lion too."

MORENA: "how is that possible?"

LEO: "everything is possible in ANALASKA."

MORENA: "What do you mean?"

LEO: "The time will tell you everything. Now, can you please take me back to the kingdom?"

MORENA: "Off course!!!"

MORENA helped LEO and they both got back to their kingdom. When she reached back to the kingdom, she saw AAZARO waiting for her in the hall. She ran towards him and hugged him. AAZARO pushed her in angry manner.

AAZARO: "Where the hell were you?"

MORENA: "I was just . . . ."

AAZARO: "Did you feel necessary to inform anyone here that where you are going?"

MORENA: "I . . . ."

AAZARO (IN LOUDER WAY): "Tell me, did you inform anyone?"

MORENA: "NO, MY LORD."

AAZARO: "How dare you, how you can be so careless? I gave you a big responsibility to manage the kingdom; I thought you will take care of this kingdom in well manner in my absence but you so irresponsible. Actually you know what, this is my mistake that I trusted you, you don't deserve this post, now just leave. PLEASE!!!"

MORENA: "AAZARO just listen to me please."

AAZARO (SHOUTING): "Just get out of here!!!!"

Tears came in the eyes of MORENA and she ran toward her home. She didn't talk to anyone but she was crying, the night came but tears didn't stop. At mid of the night, LEO came to her room. LEO was watching her from the balcony and called her in sign language.

MORENA came near to him and helped him to come to her room, LEO came to her room.

MORENA: "What are you doing here?"

LEO: "Actually, today someone helped me when I was groaning in pain. So, how can I leave that person when she is in pain?"

MORENA: "Who said that I am in pain, I am totally fine." LEO wiped out her tears and said, "either you are telling a lie or your tears, I think this time MISS. MORENA is telling a lie because theses precious tears can't come out without any reason." MORENA (SMILED) said, "You are incorrigible."

LEO: "Mainly, that I am."

MORENA: "What are you doing here?"

LEO: "This is the second time you are asking the same question."

MORENA: "Oh! I am so sorry, actually I was little bit tensed."

LEO: "I guess, in tension you must have not eaten anything."

MORENA: "Ah!!! Actually, I was not willing to eat anything."

LEO: "Come on, today is the full moon night . . . . let me show you one thing."

MORENA: "Where are you taking me?"

LEO: "In the jungle!!!!"

MORENA: "What, Are you mad? I can't come, mother will wake up."

LEO: "DON'T WORRY!!!!! Just come with me quietly." They both came out of the room.

MORENA: "Wait, let me take ALMAS."

LEO: "When a lion is here then why do you want take horse ride."

MORENA: "Anyone can see us."

LEO: "This is the mid-night, everyone is sleeping except us." They both laughed and LEO changed himself into lion again. MORENA sat on him and they both moved in the jungle.

THE THALOUS RIVER

The tears were gone. For the first time in life, MORENA was taking ride of a lion. They both reached a place where the full moon was visible. MORENA jumped from him and walked towards the full moon. LEO turned himself to a man again. Suddenly, MORENA saw a shining thing in front of her. She turned back to LEO but he was not there and she started calling him.

MORENA: "LEO, LEO . . . . LEO!!!! Where you are gone?" She again turned and saw LEO preparing a table.

MORENA: "Where you were gone, and what are you doing?"

LEO: "I guess, MISS. MORENA is hungry because she has not eaten anything since evening." MORENA was quite.

LEO: "Please, young lady sit here."

MORENA sat on the chair and in her front LEO sat down. MORENA saw LEO has prepared a big hill of her favorite fruits.

MORENA: "How do you know that I like these fruits? I thought you must be non-vegetarian."

LEO: "Why? Is it prohibited for the lion to eat fruits and I don't know whether you like these fruits or not, but I like these fruits very much." They both began eating the dinner. After they finish they were sitting at bridge like place.

MORENA: "Hey which place is this, it seems like there must be a river and that hill looks like a water fall hill."

LEO: "Actually, this is the place where a magical river used to flow, you know in that river beautiful mermaids used to live and that place where you think was water fall place, was really that place."

MORENA: "Then where all those things gone, I mean where all those mermaids are gone and why this place has become drought place."

LEO: "I don't know and I don't think anyone knows about it, I guess more than 20 years have been passed away and this place is still the same."

MORENA: "I want to know the truth, can you please tell me how and why this place became like this."

LEO: "I will try my level best but I don't think that anyone must know about this river."

MORENA: "It's ok, but try it and I think we should move towards our homes again because morning is about to arrive."

LEO: "Why not my princes!!!!! LEO again turned back into a lion and MORENA sat on him and they both went back to their homes." The next morning when MORENA opened her doors, she saw her mother standing, her mother hugged her and said, "my baby, I am sorry my baby, I didn't understand anything."

MORENA: "I am fine mother, I am fine."

VAROCIA: "See this!!!"

She handed her a letter written by AAZARO, requesting her to join her duty again and seeking for her forgiveness. MORENA wrote another letter to him in which she wrote her feelings.

My LORD AAZARO,

Kindly pardon me, but I don't think I will be able to join the duty again as I had been regarded as an irresponsible person. I don't think that there is less number of people who are not wise as me. So, please don't ask me to join the post again. In your absence, I performed my duty with full devotion but you were not able to see that and I can't listen anything against my self-respect. I tried to persuade you, I tried all my levels to make you happy but you didn't allow me to do so. I hope you will work better without me.

All the best my LORD.

Yours truly,
MORENA

She handled this letter to a guard and sent it to AAZARO. When he read the letter he realized what he has done with her. He was in his balcony and this letter was kept on his bed when ALBERT CRUZ entered, he took up the letter and read it out; after he read that letter, secretly he came near to AAZARO and began to talk to him.

ALBERT CRUZ: "Why are you doing this AAZARO?"

AAZARO: "What have I done now?"

ALBERT CRUZ: "You know it very well what I am talking about."

AAZARO: "But I am not willing to talk about it."

ALBERT CRUZ: "Fine, I am not going to force you to talk to me about your personal matter, but without talking you can't find the answers of your questions."

AAZARO: "Please, explain what are trying to say."

ALBERT CRUZ: "A time was there, when your father was facing the same condition, when your mother was in love with him and he was escaping from his feelings."

AAZARO: "My father was escaping, but why?"

ALBERT CRUZ: "Your father lost his parents in a very mysterious mishap, in a very young age, from then he took the responsibility of this kingdom but never allowed anyone to come near to him but destiny is destiny."

AAZARO: "Getting love from mother was the destiny."

ALBERT CRUZ: "No my dear, but getting a beautiful person in his life who never let you feel alone or hapless was his destiny. Those open wounds of your father was only filled by the love of your mother, his loneliness was gone and he began to feel happy and he realized that he has fallen in love with a girl and you know what he did the same thing as you did with MORENA but your method was quite different.",

AAZARO: "I don't love her."

ALBERT CRUZ: "Really, then this news is not important for you."

AAZARO: "What news?"

ALBERT CRUZ: "Actually, it was about her but leave it I will see her."

AAZARO: "What happened? I mean is everything all right, she is fine or not, any bad omen or anything else. Please, tell me everything is fine or not?"

ALBERT CRUZ: "Why you are bothering, it's not your matter, she is a mere mob girl."

AAZARO (shouting): "How dare you to call her a mere mob girl."

ALBERT CRUZ: "Why not she is a mere mob girl?"

AAZARO: "She is not so!!!"

ALBERT CRUZ: "Then who is she?"

AAZARO: "Because she is mine."

ALBERT CRUZ: "I know you love her."

AAZARO: "I don't think that I love her or even deserve such kind of girl".

ALBERT CRUZ: "AAZARO the same tension, the same feelings and the same love for you I have seen in her eyes also. When you were not here, I saw that girl visiting your room at every hour and going near to the balcony to see whether you have come or not. Her eyes always look forward for your arrival, she wanted you to come out of thoughts and stressed and I realized that she was the only one in this palace who understood your pain and tried her all the levels to make you happy. And, I also saw you avoiding her and making her unsuccessful in all her techniques."

AAZARO: "Because I didn't want to be a black cloud on her life. I am a bad omen and I don't want her to get hurt because of me. Earlier also something has happened to her because of me. You know what, she was about to lose her life. I really don't want this."

ALBERT CRUZ: "A girl who saved your life after making her life going in danger, you made her cry in front of whole palace, was this your justice my lord?"

AAZARO: "ALBERT, don't make me feel ashamed on myself."

ALBERT CRUZ: "You should feel it. But this is not the right time for all these things. You need to say sorry to her and tell your feelings too."

AAZARO: "I can't, I did wrong, very wrong and I think, I have lost my friendship too."

ALBERT CRUZ: "Then, this is the perfect time to gain it and try to console her and then tell her your feelings."

AAZARO: "Do you think she will understand and will forgive me."

ALBERT CRUZ: "As I have seen, she will surely forgive because she loves you."

AAZARO hugged ALBERT and said, "If my father would have been alive, then he must have understood my feelings like you. Thank you sir!!!"

ALBERT CRUZ: "I am always there for you my son." Now, go and get her. AAZARO left the palace and went to MORENA'S home. But she was not there. VAROCIA told him that she has gone somewhere to practice for archery. Then AAZARO understood where she has gone. On the other hand, MORENA was walking on the path where she went in the mid night with LEO. She was walking on that path and when she reached their, she again started searching for that shinning thing that she saw yesterday. Looking here and there, eventually her eyes went on that shinning thing again which was in the just at midst. She went near to that thing and sat down; she was staring at that piece. It was looking like a broken piece of a sword, when MORENA was to touch that broken piece, she saw something that was quite horrible, and she saw again a giant man killing MORENA by a huge sword. Seeing such vicious vision she pulled her hands and stood up. She began to walk far from that piece, but her interest to know the secret behind her visions again made her to go near to the broken piece. She ran towards it and she took out the piece, for fraction of seconds everything was quiet and then the place began to shiver, suddenly MORENA saw the place from where she took out the piece that shivered and huge amount of water came out of it. It was looking like a water fall, MORENA just ran towards the edge and saw that that water fall leading to opposite flow of the river, that sear area and the main waterfall which was on mountain . . . . just began to flow when opposite river started.

The whole water was flowing in opposite direction and suddenly from that hole many mermaids came out, they were jumping and swimming, the river was shining like a beautiful diamond, it was looking as if someone has left many diamonds in the river and the bright sun is making them to shine. The mermaids came near to the edge and began to talk to MORENA.

MERMAID: "Who are you and how you did this?"

MORENA: "my name is MORENA, I am the daughter of CAPRION and VAROCIA, and who are you?"

MERMAID: "My name is YURA and these are my friends; are you sure that you are the daughter of CAPRION and VAROCIA?"

MORENA: "Yes, do have any problem?"

YURA: "No, actually the thing is, that broken piece of sword which you pulled that can't be pulled up by a mere human."

MORENA: "So, what do you think, I am the daughter of whom?"

When she asked this question to all of them, they all went back to the river and suddenly MORENA heard the sound of horse hoods. She turned back and saw AAZARO. He got off the horse and came near to MORENA.

AAZARO: "This river?, it was not here earlier.",

MORENA: "Yes, it was not here." She showed him the broken piece of the sword and said, "last night I came here and this shinning broken piece, I don't know why but I wanted to take this, so, I came here and when I pulled this, all of a sudden back flowing river began to flow. And, you know what . . . . There are many mermaids in this."

AAZARO: "This River is shining a lot; I mean this was the only thing left to complete the beauty of this jungle. But I have not come here to praise this river."

MORENA: "Then for what you have come here my lord."

AAZARO: "Please MORENA!!!!! Don't say this, I am feeling ashamed on myself. I know, I did wrong with you but there were certain reasons behind it, I can explain you everything, just listen to me."

When he was speaking, MORENA felt he was stammering and she suddenly kissed him. It was the evening time, just like their first kiss scenario. She was holding his hairs and his shoulder and he was just holding her waist, they were so close as if they don't want to leave each other. At the back, the backward river was flowing, the mermaids too were seeing this beautiful scene and they were jumping, the sun was just making the river to shine and both of them too, the greenery and all the things around was just admiring both of them. When she stopped she said, "I have told you earlier, if you are able to forgive yourself for your mistake then God forgives you and I am a mere human.

AAZARO (KISSING AGAIN AND HOLDING HER): "I never expected that someone would understand me so nicely and would forgive me without any complaints. My heart was right, I am sorry."

MORENA (KISSING HIM AGAIN): "You don't have to be sorry, your eyes say everything to me (touching his heart), and your heart beats told everything to me. I realized AAZARO, I felt your feelings in me in your absence, I don't know what this is but I missed you a lot, I mean my heart says that . . . ."

AAZARO kept his finger on her lips and said that he can't survive without her beats which lies in me. Tears came out of her eyes and they both hugged each other. Suddenly, MORENA felt something like this has happened earlier too and that nightmare again came in front of her eyes, this time more vicious, she saw herself and AAZARO getting killed by someone whom she knows but they were killed at different places. She pushed AAZARO and turned towards the sun and began to whoop.

AAZARO: "Again those nightmares?"

He came near to her and stood at her back, he moved his one hand and kept it on her heart and his second hand was holding her waist, his lips were touching her ears and then he said, "you possess my heart beats, I can't run away from you. I feel you in my each breath, I can't breathe without you, and your existence in my life is like blood in my veins. I can't say that my life is impossible without you but I can say I am incomplete without you, you complete me, if you want to be afraid then get afraid but don't get afraid of me, because I am you and you are me, I reside in your heart and you reside in me, I LOVE YOU MORENA!!!!!", The pearl eyes with tears just began to stare AAZARO'S eyes and wanted to speak something but in speechless manner.

AAZARO: "I can't see tears in your eyes." She wiped out her tears and kept her hands on his hands and said, "I LOVE YOU, AAZARO!!!!! My life is just like this sear river without you."

AAZARO: "I know."

She turned towards him and they both kissed each other again and they moved towards the unicorn. When they were leaving, YURA came back and called MORENA and asked, "Don't you want to name this river?"

AAZARO: "You made this river to flow again so you should decide the name and this is my order."

MORENA (smiled): "THALOUS RIVER."

AAZARO: "Quite interesting my love." YURA and all the mermaids just took the zest and again got back to river and they both also got on the unicorn and began to move to the palace. When they reached the palace everyone saw MORENA and AAZARO together, they all got a huge shock and they all became speechless. AAZARO got down of the horse and held MORENA'S hand and helped her to get down while holding her hands, he took her inside the palace and called all the important people and in front of all of them he bend down on his knees and asked MORENA to forgive him.

AAZARO: "In front of the whole kingdom, I blamed for the thing that you didn't do. So, today in front of all of them I am asking for your forgiveness, kindly forgive me Miss. MORENA, the great advisor of the ANALASKA.",

MORENA (holding the hands and making him to stand): "My lord!!! You don't have to be sorry, you realized your mistake that's enough for me, and I have forgiven you. So, please, don't embarrass me."

ALBERT CRUZ: "It's quite good to see the advisor of the kingdom, back again in the palace."

AAZARO: "I have to make an important announcement, at the end of jungle where earlier a river used to flow and due to some reasons it became sear but today because of MORENA that river has begun to flow again in backward direction. From today, that river will be called as THALOUS RIVER."

ALBERT CRUZ: "What did you say, that river which was sear has begun to flow again, but how?"

AAZARO: "There is a very lengthy story and we all have enough work to do. So, let's complete the work first."

AEYRENA: "AAZARO and MORENA, you both don't know that it's not a mere river but it's a magical river."

MORENA—AAZARO: "MAGICAL RIVER?"

ALBERY CRUZ: "Yes, didn't you see that river flows in the backward direction. It goes down to up, it's not like mere rivers that flows from up to down. You know there are many mermaids and that river always shines like a diamond. Hardly matters its day or night or the night without moon. That river always shines."

MORENA: "Yes, I have seen that, that river shines a lot."

AEYRENA: "From now onwards, THALOUS River has divided this kingdom in real two forms."

AAZARO: "Yes, I have seen, but ALBERT tells what the last destination of this river is?"

ALBERT: "Till now it's a mystery, this river was not able to get its destination and till today it must be flowing to get its destination and when the river will get its destination, this river will begin to flow in the normal river direction."

MORENA: "Why? MR. ALBERT, I mean how is this possible that a river flowing from such long way became sear in search of its destination."

AEYRENA: "No, MORENA, at that time that river didn't get its destination and it didn't become sear in search of the destination but due to some other reasons it became sear."

AAZARO: "What was the reason?"

ALBERT: "No one knows, I think no one in this kingdom have any idea about it.

MORENA: "But, how it is possible that no one have any idea about it, I mean that river used to flow once and suddenly it became sear, such large river, how can this be possible that no one has seen this incident while it was happening."

AEYRENA: "It's being told to us that those people who saw this incident, they became blind, then and their only. And after few days, they died. This is a mystery till today that river is searching its destination."

AAZARO: "This is a very big mystery. I hope that this incident is not going to repeat again." MORENA was quite tensed about the incident; the words of ALBERT AND AEYRENA forced her mind to think about the incident when she was pulling the broken piece. She was in the balcony of AAZARO, while thinking she didn't realize that AAZARO has entered in the room. He secretly entered in the room and hold MORENA and asked, "Thinking about me?" She became shocked and turn towards him.

MORENA: "NO, I mean yes, I mean no."

AAZARO: "No, yes, MISS. ADVISOR firstly be justified with your answer."

MORENA: "I am sorry, I was just thinking about that."

AAZARO: "What, about THALOUS?"

MORENA: "How do you know?"

AAZARO: "I knew this thing, since when I saw the signs of tension on my love's face, in the hall."

MORENA: "So, you read the faces too!!!"

AAZARO: "Actually, only of yours. As you understand me, before I speak"

MORENA: "I have to go home, it's getting late." She began to move and AAZARO hold her hands and pulled her towards him.

AAZARO (HOLDING HER SO TIGHTLY): "I know it's getting late, but I think the advisor is getting late not my love!!!"

MORENA: "REALLY, I think your love is a girl and daughter of someone too, I need to get back to my house." She was trying to move and suddenly he leaves her and then MORENA turns to kiss him and then she says, "Good bye!!!!!" She leaves the room and move towards her house. It seemed as if today is the happiest day of MORENA'S and AAZARO'S life but excess happiness always gives the sign of a big bang upcoming sorrow. When she reached home, her behavior was very strange compared to the other days. She behaved with her parents in a childish manner and then she entered in the room, she was smiling without any reason and then she fallen down on her bed. While lying on the bed too, she was smiling and then she realized that she has to take bath as she daily take twice in a day. She took bath and came near to the mirror, she was looking herself in very different manner, and it was like she is admiring herself. When she was doing such things, she noticed a very abnormal thing; she saw her golden hand turning to a normal human nerve. She became shocked, she saw her upper portion hand nerves have turned to a normal human nerves. She put back her clothes and got in the cob webs of questions. She lied down on her bed and began to think again, then a new thought came to her mind and she started murmuring, "my nerves are changing their color, it means I am becoming a normal human, so what I was earlier, no, no, I think I must be having these nerves as a bad omen, now the time is changing for me, now I can live my life as a normal human with my love." She was smiling and the same thing was happening with AAZARO. He also saw his nerves and got the same thought as MORENA had. The bright night with full moon came, they were lost in each other's dream, and neither MORENA had her dinner or AAZARO. In the mid night when she was about to fall asleep, she heard the sound of parrot coming from her balcony, she came near to that beautiful white and red parrot who was saying something, "MORENA, I love you, you are my everything, I am waiting for you.",

MORENA: "What is your name, and who loves me, I mean who is waiting for Me.", the parrot flied and MORENA just bend down little bit and saw AAZARO standing downstairs. She saw AAZARO in a very handsome look, that time he was really looking like a guy to whom she began to love; he was not at all looking like a king.

MORENA: "AAZARO, what are you doing here?"

AAZARO: "Actually, I was missing you. So, I thought to see you."

MORENA: "You saw me, now go back to palace, anyone can see you, just go now."

AAZARO: "Actually, I wanted to show you something."

MORENA: "What?"

AAZARO: "For that you have to come with me."

MORENA: "Fine, but I can't come now."

AAZARO: "This is the only time, when I can show you this thing."

MORENA: "Just wait, I am coming." MORENA made a long rope of some clothes, with the help of which she came down and AAZARO held her. They both on the same horse went to the palace. He quietly took her on the roof of the palace.

MORENA: "In the morning also you can show me this thing, which you really want to show me now."

AAZARO: "Just close your eyes!!!"

MORENA: "Why, do I look more beautiful while becoming blind?"

AAZARO kissed her both the eyes calmly and the eyes itself got closed, he took her in his arms and she hold him, he kept on saying, "don't you dare to open your eyes!!!!!" He just came near to the edge of the roof and got her down from his arms and again holds her smoothly and said, "Now open your pearl eyes." Slowly and gradually she opened her eyes, she saw a fairy tale like scene, she saw the THALOUS RIVER in front of her, the whole ANALASKA was looking as if it was wrapped by a shining cover and the full moon light was brightening the whole kingdom, the trees, the flowers and the houses were shining so much.

MORENA: "Wow, I have never ever seen such magical scene."

AAZARO: "Really? But there is something else too that I want to show you."

MORENA: "Something more beautiful than this?"

AAZARO: "You are the most beautiful my love, but less than your beauty . . . . there is something I got to show you."

MORENA: "What else?"

AAZARO: "Just give me a second." He whistled ALMAS, and on that time MORENA, for the very first time, saw that unicorn with wings. He came on the roof by flying and came near to them.

MORENA: "ALMAS, you have wings? How did I never notice such beautiful wings of yours?"

AAZARO: "Today, whatever you did for mermaids. They wanted to say thanks to you. So, for that they have given wings to your unicorn as a gift to you. Come, we need to move now." They both sat on the unicorn and they flew, they saw their kingdom from the top while flying in the beautiful sky, it was looking so magical and beautiful while they both were together and were kept smiling. They both reached at the river again, but at the apex of the river. They both were standing at the edge of the hill, where that river was coming in the opposite direction; there was a tree whose leaves were in golden and red color. In the presence of the full moon light, that river and that tree were shining a lot and was spreading an incredible bling in the environment, ALMAS came down near the tree, it was all looking very beautiful, the surrounding was totally green and many night flowers were blooming. They both came down and went under the groove of the tree. This time something was different, the waves in the river was so high and its speed was very fast. They both were standing under the groove of the tree when AAZARO held the hands of MORENA and pointed towards the sky, where many glow worms were making the full moon light more romantic.

MORENA: "AAZARO, when did you think of all these things? I mean this situation, I have never ever seen something like this in my life, and this is so beautiful and so pious."

AAZARO: "Did you like this?"

MORENA (with a cute smile): "Off course!!!! I love this."

They both sat just beneath the tree, AAZARO supported his back with the help of the tree and MORENA took support of him, she kept her face near his heart and held his hands and was admiring each other. They were quite. It seemed as if their eyes were talking, her eyes were staring him and his eyes were answering the questions that were rising from her eyes. The atmosphere was so quiet and so beautiful, that they both were lost in each other. After an hour they both fell asleep. ALMAS was near to them and taking care of them. MORENA again saw that nightmare. This time she felt the agony, she saw a very beautiful woman crying and it was quite shocking to see that, that woman was holding the dead body of MORENA at some very beautiful and strange place. It was not looking like EARTH but something else. Then, she saw that her dead body is falling from high edge of some mountain into some river and after that, that river became sear. She again woke up in hurry and began to whoop due to which AAZARO also woke up.

AAZARO: "MORENA? Are you fine? What happened? That nightmare again came?" She hugged him as tightly as a child hugs someone when he is afraid.

MORENA: "I really don't know, why I see these nightmares but these nightmares frightens me a lot. AAZARO I am still afraid, are these nightmares symbolizing something to me that I am not able to see or are these giving me hints about my future?"

AAZARO: "Do you love me?"

MORENA: "Now, what kind of question is this?"

AAZARO: "I know the answer is yes."

MORENA: "When you know the answer, then why are you asking me this?"

AAZARO: "Just confirming!!!! I am waiting for the day when my love will going to bound you in all manners and will take you in such beautiful world, where you will be mine . . . . only mine!!!! Free of everything, where no nightmares would be there to frighten you, I will take you to my world . . . . just allow me once and love me, just trust our love MORENA for once. I promise you that no one will scare you except me."

This time she kept her hand on his heart and said, "I can be miss guided by the words of yours, but not by the heart beats of mine that resides in you. I know this heart will never lie to me, I trust our love more than myself, AAZARO. MY AAZARO!!!!!" When AAZARO listened her words he held her hands softly and kissed her. Again, in the romantic atmosphere they were lost and then they hugged. ALMAS began to point towards the sun and they both understood that they have to move towards their houses.

AAZARO: "Not willing to leave you?"

MORENA: "You are saying as if it's easy for me to leave you."

AAZARO: "Let's move before the sun rises." They both got up and sat on ALMAS and he took both of them to the kingdom. In the morning the kingdom was looking as if, it was wrapped in the fog."

MORENA: "It's looking like winters are approaching."

AAZARO: "I just love winters, because it is the only time when I used to miss you a lot."

MORENA: "OH! Really? This king lies a lot." They both got down from the unicorn; it was MORENA'S house where they got down.

MORENA: "MY LORD, please take ALMAS with you, he will drop you safely to the palace."

AAZARO: "OH! Really? Is he that better?"

MORENA: "Yes, he can love you in a better manner than me."

AAZARO: "Really? Then I should love him rather than loving you."

MORENA: "Why not? So from now onwards I will help you to love him."

AAZARO (PULLED HER TOWARDS HIM): "It's better, at least by this means I can have more time to spend with you."

MORENA: "Just leave me before someone sees us like this."

AAZARO: "Let the people see, how much I love you."

MORENA: "This misbehaves don't suits on a king."

AAZARO: "With MORENA, AAZARO IS ONLY AAZARO, A MERE AAZARO WHO LOVES HIS LOVE SO MUCH. WITH YOU, I DON'T CONSIDER MYSELF AS A KING."

MORENA: "Just stop trapping me in your love web and go now."

AAZARO: "Fine, I am going. Meet you after few hours."

MORENA: "YES MY LORD, I MEAN AAZARO, MY AAZARO." AAZARO went to the palace and got back to his room and slept. While sleeping he didn't realize how time passed away and that day no one came to his room also to disturb him except his love MORENA. She was also quite late for her work; she went to the minister's room ALBERT CRUZ.

MORENA: "Good morning MR. ALBERT."

ALBERT: "Good morning my daughter. Are you ok?"

MORENA: "Yes, I am totally fine!!!!! Why do you ask me such question?"

ALBERT: "For the first time you came late to the palace, that's why I asked."

MORENA: "Where is our lord? I can't see him anywhere."

ALBERT: "You will not find him anywhere except his room."

MORENA: "Is he still sleeping?"

ALBERT: "Maybe!!! I don't know." When MORENA heard that AAZARO is still sleeping, she silently went near to the door of his room and took out her sword. Then she quietly entered in the room. Her thought was right he was sleeping, in fact sleeping very deeply. MORENA quietly pointed her sword towards his neck and suddenly AAZARO opened his eyes. He held the sword from the back without seeing her and pulled the sword towards him; he snatched the sword from her and made her to fall down on bed under him.

MORENA (BREATHING DEEPLY): "I was just checking, weather a warrior is sleeping or a lazy man!!!"

AAZARO (BREATHING DEEPLY): "Now what your prediction says MISS. ADVISOR?"

AAZARO was just willing to kiss her and he was getting more close to her when MORENA said, "MR. ALBERT!!!" AAZARO turned and MORENA got out of the clutches of his powerful arms.

MORENA: "Now my prediction says, that the king should be more flexible and need to do more practice of the lessons that he has learnt in the quest."

AAZARO: "Really?"

MORENA: "Yes!!!! Off course!!!! Now get ready my lord, this is not the time to sleep. This is the time of a king not AAZARO'S." They both chuckled and MORENA came out of the room while AAZARO was getting ready.

That was like an important day, because on that very day all the important people of ANALASKA were gathered in the hall and waiting for AAZARO to come and start the important conference. When AAZARO entered in the hall, all of them got up from their royal chairs in order to give respect to AAZARO. AAZARO went near to the throne and sat on it, and asked everybody to sit.

AAZARO: "I was being informed that you all want to consult some problems with me regarding our kingdom. Can I have CAPRION to reveal the matter?"

CAPRION: "My lord, from quite some time I have been looking this kingdom very carefully and found something very strange and bad."

AAZARO: "Please!!!! CAPRION, tell me the whole matter."

CAPRION: "From few days, I am getting the complains of kidnapping and lost people from the mob. And I found, in our army the soldiers are getting less, even I got the news from our neighboring kingdom i.e. THE ZUERO'S KINGDOM that their oldest vision teller DEDALLION is missing.

AAZARO: "DEDALLION? I have met her, she is lost, she was quite young and how this can be possible?"

ALBERT CRUZ: "One more shocking thing is left my lord."

AAZARO: "What else?"

ALBERT CRUZ: "Yesterday, I visited PIERO and found few graveyards opened. Those graves were not of any mere person or any mere prisoners; it was of those prisoners who had committed sins."

AAZARO: "I think, this not a simple matter"

AAZARO stood up from his throne and said, "we all need to be more careful, from now onwards their will three parts of the kingdom and these three parts will be seen by three different people, the jungle area will be looked forward by CAPRION, the residential area will be looked up by ALBERT CRUZ and all the secret paths and secret things in the kingdom will be looked up by MISS. MORENA and these 3 portions will be under my control and every day I will look forward for the work of yours, everyone please be careful. If it is that what I am thinking, then attacks will take place again. We have to be careful. In the night only, this thing will happen."

MORENA: "How you can be so sure?"

AAZARO: "Because evil will not come in sunlight as their power decreases during day time and people will figure them out. Their powers increase with the night, and the darkness is the main source of power for them. We all need to be very active and careful during night time."

CAPRION: "We promise!!!!! We will do it. But we really don't have any idea with whom our real fight is."

MORENA: "That's what, we have to find out."

We all will be on our positions from today onwards. That day was the full moon night and all of them were at their positions, MORENA was at the secret paths, ALBERT was looking after the residential area and the jungle area was looked forward by CAPRION. AAZARO had taken approximate 3 rounds of the kingdom and looking forward for the attack. But except CAPRION, no one faced anything. While moving in the jungle, CAPRION reached at the place near the river. He went near the river to drink water and he started drinking water from the river. While he was washing the face, he felt someone else face in the river and shockingly he moved back, he asked himself, "what was it?", He took out his sword and stood and again went near to the river. As he was getting near to the edge, he heard the voice of an animal, he stopped and bends down. Suddenly, a giant, vicious and very cruel werewolf with bat wings jumped over him, that werewolf crossed him, CAPRION fell down and turned and saw a dark night black werewolf with batwings and vampire teeth's. He was shocked; he had never ever seen such vicious animal. He got sacred, that giant and vicious vampire werewolf was roaring and looking at CAPRION in very cruel manner. The fight began and the werewolf was getting dominant over CAPRION. He was quite powerful and vicious and his attacks were highly dangerous. When, he attacked on CAPRION, at that time CAPRION fell down, he fainted and that werewolf came on him, he raised his hands to kill CAPRION but suddenly at that instant, AAZARO reached over there on RUBIZN and shot the eyes of that werewolf; that werewolf got hurt through the arrow, he moved back and roared and went back in the river. AAZARO got down from his unicorn and ran towards CAPRION, he came near to him and kept his head on his lap, he touched his nerves, and fortunately it was working; AAZARO found CAPRION being alive, he kept him on his shoulder and then kept him on his unicorn and they both moved back to the palace.

The morning came all the members returned to their home. When MORENA returned to her home, she found her house opened; no one was there. She became shocked. She ran and took ALMAS and moved towards the palace. Her face was showing the sign of tension, she reached the palace and entered in the palace, and she ran near to AAZARO'S room and saw AAZARO consoling VAROCIA.

MORENA: "Mother, what you are doing here?" They both hugged and MORENA saw VAROCIA crying.

MORENA: "Tell me; what's wrong, why you are crying?"

VAROCIA: "MORENA, YOUR FATHER!!!"

MORENA: "What happened to father? Mother, tell me?" AAZARO came near to her and held her hands; he took her to the room where he was kept. MORENA went near to him, his hands were full of marks, and he was quite faint. Tears came in her eyes. AAZARO comforted her by hugging.

MORENA: "AAZARO, who did this? What was that? These marks can't be made by a mere human."

AAZARO: "You are right; I saw that, it was not a mere human but a vampire werewolf with bat wings." At that instant ALBERT CRUZ just entered in the room. ALBERT: "Did I hear a vampire werewolf with bat wings?"

AAZARO: "Yes, you have heard it right"

ALBERT: "Was he dark black in color?"

AAZARO: "Yes!!!"

ALBERT: "Was his eyes were dark red?"

AAZARO: "Yes!!!"

ALBERT: "Did he look scary and giant?"

AAZARO: "Yes!!! But how do you know all these things?"

ALBERT: "Oh my god!!!!! He woke up!!!!"

MORENA: "Who woke up and what are you trying to say?"

ALBERT: "VOLVO!!!!"

AAZARO and MORENA: "VOLVO, who is this?"

ALBERT: "He woke up from PIERO."

AAZARO: "PIERO, but it is the graveyard of prisoners, so how can an animal? ALBERT will tell me everything."

ALBERT: "I never ever thought that he will come back."

MORENA: "ALBERT, please tell us who is he?"

ALBERT: "His name is Volvo, he was a prisoner, once he tried to ran, and he was also about to be successful but in the jungle the same type werewolf bitten him, and that werewolf died and VOLVO became faint. He was caught by the soldiers and they threw him in the prison. When the night came, he woke up and began to shout, he was shouting a lot. Listening this sound, the soldiers came inside the prison and they saw him lying at the floor, he was looking different, his hands hided his face but when a soldier was about to touch his, he raised his hand and held his neck, his face became like the same werewolf, he threw the soldier on the floor and came out of the prison, he was very disturbed. He was not able to walk properly. Slowly and gradually, he was turning to a vampire werewolf, the bat wings also appeared on his back.

AAZARO: "If he was successful in running, then how he was buried in PIERO."

ALBERT: "Your father killed him; the king of the kingdom killed him."

AAZARO: "But how he killed him?"

ALBERT: "Back in time people were getting kidnaped as they are now, he was not killing them but sucking their blood at every full moon night. Many complains were coming and being the king he has to do something."

MORENA: "Then, what he did?"

ALBERT: "I have told you earlier about the sword that you have, it can kill any evil in this world. With the help of this sword only, your father killed him."

MORENA: "If he was killed and buried, then how did he come back? Did you all check properly when he was killed? I mean when you buried, might be he was not dead, he was acting and on the next full night he might have, and woke up again."

ALBERT: "Any evil in this world can't be saved, if he is attacked by this sword."

AAZARO: "But how he was killed?"

MORENA: "We don't have enough time for this; we have to be very careful now. If he has really come back, then he is not going to be silent; he will fulfill his thrust."

ALBERT: "MORENA and AAZARO, always remember one thing that the evils in whatever form they are . . . . they also had to follow their rules and regulations."

MORENA: "Are you serious? Do evils follow any rules and regulations?"

ALBERT: "Everything which exists in this nature follows their rules and regulations."

AAZARO: "Ok, he is hurt. I don't think his attack will be seen very soon."

MORENA: "He is hurt; this means his next attack will be more dangerous. Since, you hurt him this means his next attack will be on you."

AAZARO: "I am waiting for that!!!"

When the conversation got over AAZARO had something in his mind. He went in his rooms and began to think over all the mysterious crimes happening in the kingdom but his thinking level wasn't able to go far beyond the things that were happening; being a king he had the strong feeling that because of VOLVO these crimes are happening but this was not the main reason. In the mid-evening he asked everybody to gather in the hall. All the important members gathered in the hall and AAZARO sat on throne. The attack on CAPRION was being shared with everybody and solution was asked. All of them were giving their opinion but still AAZARO was not able to concentrate and he was just trying to focus on only one thing, "why VOLVO attacked on CAPRION so brutally, what was his motto?" Then he began to think over the words of MORENA that he will be his next prey but AAZARO had the feeling that the attack will not be done on him but on someone who is for him. This was the thing which was troubling him but he wasn't able to understand who will be that person because there are many people in the kingdom to whom he loves and the most important thing was that that he didn't have any idea that how VOLVO can be killed. The method was known by his father who was dead and no one else had any idea regarding this.

MORENA said, "Please, everyone be silent!!!!! Yours this behavior can't lead to any solution, my lord what do think what we should do?", AAZARO stood up from the throne and said, "from now onwards I will appoint the soldiers over those places where I appointed three of them until I find the solution of the problem and don't worry, I will be doing my job in the same way as I was doing it with them. I want to claim this thing in the kingdom that everyone needs to be more careful. In the nights, I request all the people not to roam in the kingdom anywhere not even in their courtyards until and unless the problem is solved. I hope you all understand my meaning.", after saying this AAZARO walked out and everybody left the hall.

MORENA saw the reaction of everyone and she understood that AAZARO has caught in his thoughts, he needs guidance. She went to ALBERT CRUZ'S room and asked him to guide AAZARO. ALBERT understood MORENA, and went to the room of AAZARO to talk to him.

ALBERT: "The king is quite busy in his thoughts!!!!" AAZARO was standing in his balcony and was looking onto his kingdom.

AAZARO: "I am fine but someone is taking more worries for me, am I right ALBERT?" ALBERT laughed and came near to him and said, "I know you are quite tensed but tension can give rise to a new tension but not solution. Listen to me VOLVO is hurt and he went back.... I don't think he will return at all because he must not be willing to die again. So, don't take tension."

AAZARO: "Are you sure, you think so?"

ALBERT: "I know this very well."

AAZARO: "But a king can't think so easily, like you."

ALBERT: "So after being a king and complicating things, did you find any answer?"

AAZARO: "No not at all. In fact, the more I chase answers, the more I'm getting trapped in the web of the questions."

ALBERT: "My son, don't think so much. Just relax this is time for you to spend with someone else, who is very special to you and who needs you this time a lot." AAZARO and ALBERT chuckled and they both left the room. MORENA was just standing at the door of the room and she was hiding herself. When they both came out, ALBERT went to his room and AAZARO was just standing beside MORENA. She thought that he is not able to see her, but as ALBERT left.... suddenly AAZARO held her hands and pulled her in the room, he held her hands and she was trying to get rid of him. He held her hands so tightly, that she wasn't able to get rid of him. Without saying anything he kissed her, but at the time of kiss also she was trying to push him out, but AAZARO was not leaving her at all. The motion stopped and MORENA held him softly and was kissing him. They both had their long kiss for the first time and when AAZARO left he said, "thank you, thank you and I love you." MORENA kissed him again and said, "I know you love me, only."

AAZARO: "There is a place that I wanted to show you."

MORENA: "Which place and why didn't you show me that earlier?"

AAZARO: "Just waiting for the perfect time." He held her hands and took her towards the balcony and asked her, "Can you see the sky being in total pink in color?" MORENA replied, "This is beautiful!!!!" AAZARO exclaimed, "Just wait a minute!!!!!!" He went outside the room and talked something to his servant and again came back to his room. Just back to his bed there was curtain, which was hiding a mysterious door to which he opened silently after closing his room's door.

MORENA was quite shocked to see this and said, "what is this?", AAZARO asked her to close her eyes and said, "just trust me and follow me.", He took her in his arms and went through a mysterious path and when he reached he asked her to open her eyes. As she opened her eyes, she saw that she was standing just under groove of a tree which had very different flowers and those flowers began to fall on her, then AAZARO and MORENA admire and enjoyed the incredible, beautiful surrounding of that area, the atmosphere was total pink and the tree, besides which they both where standing was full of maroon leaves. The whole scenario was quite beautiful and very pleasant. The floor was full of different red and golden leaves. They sat down over there; MORENA kept her head near the heart of AAZARO and held him in very loving and romantic mood. AAZARO too bound her in his arms and they both were lost in each other, their fingers were playing with each other, their heartbeats were racing, their breathings were very calm and soothing, and they were just lost in their romantic world, they both forgot everything except this that they are in love. The sunrays were approaching near to them, the bright pink sky was just showing the different colors of love and all the flowers and the leaves were just welcoming the new born love. They both were silent and MORENA broke the silence.

MORENA: "AAZARO, why you are tensed?"

AAZARO: "I am not tensed at all."

MORENA: "No you are!!!!"

AAZARO: "How can you say that?" She got up and held his face by her hand and said, "AAZARO, you know why I hug u when u tell a lie?"

AAZARO: "Why?"

MORENA: "BECAUSE, AT THAT TIME I WANT TO LISTEN TO YOUR PIOUS HEART . . . . WHAT HE IS TRYING TO SPEAK, I WANT TO FEEL YOUR EACH AND EVERY BREATH THAT WHAT IT'S TELLING ME AND I REALLY SEE IN YOUR INNOCENT EYES, WHAT THEY TRY TO REVEAL. WHATEVER YOU ARE NOT ABLE TO TELL ME OR IF YOU LIE TO ME THEN YOUR THESE THINGS COMFORT ME BY TELLING ME EVERYTHING IN SPEECHLESS MANNER." AAZARO hugged her and said, "I am worried about you. Except you, I don't have anyone left in my life to whom I can love or I can share my feelings."

MORENA: "AAZARO, our life is just bounded like a sea with its wave, and sea can never live without its wave, then why are you worrying about me? Just now, I am at the safest place of the whole earth."

AAZARO: "I promise, you will always be safe with me!!!!"

MORENA: "I know my AAZARO."

They both spent hours over there and then they moved towards the palace where they got the news that CAPRION has come back and they both ran towards the room. When MORENA reached at the door, she left the hands of AAZARO and ran towards her father, she went near to him and held his hands and said, "I knew it, my father is a warrior, he can't give up so easily."

CAPRION: "I knew that, these will be the only words of my daughter. "They all chuckled and all of them became very happy to see CAPRION back. While everyone was enjoying, AAZARO went back to his room and again began to think about the next attack of VOLVO. He saw from his balcony, that night has arrived and he has to go for rounds. He left his bed and came out of his palace and took RUBIZN along with him. While he was taking round, at that time he was more conscious about the jungle area and the river area. When he was roaming in the jungle . . . . he found the bushes shivering, he took out his sword and moved towards that bush. When he went near to that bush, he saw MORENA with ALMAS. They both laughed and MORENA said, "The king looks sacred."

AAZARO: "Really? I thought you got sacred that's why you came out of the bushes."

MORENA: "OH! Really, I thought I can accompany the king."

AAZARO: "Why not miss advisor." They both chuckled and started their journey. For few days, no crime or kidnaping took place. AAZARO and MORENA, they both felt that the words of ALBERT CRUZ were right. For many days no incident took place and MORENA and AAZARO left the night job, they both appointed their soldiers over them because they became quite sure, that VOLVO is not goanna return. After so many days in the evening AAZARO was standing in his balcony and watching his kingdom in happy manner. MORENA entered in his room and hugged him from the back.

AAZARO: "MORENA?"

MORENA: "How do you know that I came, because I came very quietly?"

AAZARO: "But your smell resides in me."

MORENA: "AAZARO!!!Ok, tell what are you seeing?"

AAZARO: "I am watching a lost thing."

MOREAN: "What lost thing?"

AAZARO: "Can't you see the peace that was gone and has now come back, the happiness which was totally lost has come back." MORENA held his hands and said, "Yes, my lord I can see that and I can also see the happiness on your face." AAZARO turned towards her and they both kissed each other. They both began to spend more time with each other, they usually used to visit at the secret place in the day time and in the night, and they used to visit the jungle near the river where they usually used to spend time with each other. They were getting very close and their love was getting deeper. While the brightness of new relation making their world brighter, but the darkness was too following them. While they were getting closer their nerves were turning to mere human nerves. The golden color was disappearing slowly and gradually. The whole hand didn't turn to a mere human nerve but slowly it was disappearing. They both forgot one thing, that the brightness is always followed by the dark night. While the romantic atmosphere was in ANALASKA, LAVINZO's kingdom was planning very vicious thing in its mind. LAVINZO was standing in his room and he was thinking something very important. JUDASE quietly entered in the room and broke the silence.

JUDASE: "What vicious things are revolving in your mind? Those bloody things are useless; I have a very strong feeling that you are not doing anything except wasting your time over your useless thoughts."

LAVINZO: "VOLVO, he is your main target?"

JUDASE: "Right!!! He is my main target but he is hurt, and he can't do anything."

LAVINZO: "JUDASE!!! He is hurt not dead."

JUDASE: "After getting such kind of reaction from AAZARO, I don't think he would really like to see him again."

LAVINZO: "Yes, you are absolutely right; he wouldn't like to see him because he wants to see someone else."

JUDASE: "What do you mean?"

LAVINZO: "I mean when someone is hurt by his opponent then he never tries to run away but he waits for the perfect time for his dangerous attack."

JUDASE: "I am not getting anything, what are you trying to say?"

LAVINZO: "What is the need of yours to understand anything? You need to understand only one thing that is I am dying to meet my blood, my saint brother AAZARO."

JUDASE: "What?"

LAVINZO: "Yes, I want to increase his happiness in my presence. I want to meet my brother; it's been so long to see him." While saying this, he passed a cunning smile to JUDASE and he also understood everything.

JUDASE: "To whom we are really going to meet?"

LAVIZNO: "Why are you in hurry? We have enough time to talk about this, but first make the preparation for our journey."

JUDASE: "Sure, my lord!!!!"

They both chuckled and moved for ANALASKA.

HALDIS

The day when LAVINZO was to arrive at ANALASKA, AAZARO was extremely happy. He was not able to express his happiness. He ran out of the palace, when he saw LAVINZO in his front. He hugged him and he hugged JUDASE too. He welcomed both of them very warmly. He got both of them and asked to take rest in their old rooms. They both went in their rooms and took rest. JUDASE was not at all aware with the plan of LAVINZO but LAVINZO had already decided everything in his mind, only practical was left.

In the night all the members of the palace gathered at the dinner table. LAVINZO was quietly observing everyone but he was more concentrated towards MORENA and AAZARO. He was watching both of them very closely and he got to know what is going on between MORENA and AAZARO. He laughed in himself but didn't utter any word. He finished his dinner and moved to his bed room. While he was going, JUDASE followed him and said, "Why you were giving sly smiles?"

LAVINZO: "JUDASE, you don't need to take so much stress. Just know only one thing that whatever I thought is appearing to be true." After saying this, he left him in dilemma. While he was moving towards his room, for one more time the destiny of LAVINZO let him to meet LORIYA. She too saw him and came near to him.

LORIYA: "It is my good luck, that I am able to meet you again."

LAVINZO: "Or this can be my good luck!!!"

LORIYA: "Well, I know my lord you must be very busy with your kingdom's work."

LAVINZO: "Hey!!! Please don't call me LORD; my name is not so bad."

LORIYA: "No, not at all, your name is very beautiful."

LAVINZO: "I never heard someone saying my name is good, you're the first one in my life."

LORIYA: "I am the first and I will remain at first only."

LAVINZO: "Can say this that I want to make you something else than number one."

LORIYA: "Please tell me that, I am dying to hear from many months." LAVINZO hold her and kissed her and even she held him and kissed him. They both were kissing but all of a sudden LAVINZO left her and went away from her. She became quite shocked, but she got his essence and she was happy with that. LAVINZO started running and he ran towards PIERO. He stopped near the gate and waited over there. He read the name PIERO and talked to himself, "This is my destination, I have come here for this work not for anything else, I can't destroy her life because I love her, love her, and I love her. I forgot that a heart resides in me too that has started loving her. That's why I need to remain away from her, I should follow my rules, I can't break them." He saw everything very quietly and began to observe PIERO and relationship of MORENA and AAZARO. But with the passage of time, he was getting near to LORIYA. Though, he was just trying to get away from her but his heart was not allowing him to do so. He was fallen in the beautiful trap of love. He was trying, but her existence broke his wall of patience. He began to talk to her and also started spending time with her but his eyes were stuck on his destination. He did never let LORIYA to come in between his destination.

One night came, when ALBERT CRUZ called AAZARO to tell him something. AAZARO went to his room and JUDASE followed him quietly. AAZARO entered in the room, he shut the doors.

AAZARO: "ALBER, why did you call me this time?"

ALBERT: "I have very important information to tell you."

AAZARO: "What important information?"

ALBERT: "You must know all the things about EBONY?"

AAZARO: "Yes, I mean that is a prisoner's jail!!!!"

ALBERT: "That's not a mere prisoner's jail, it's something else."

AAZARO: "What do you mean by that?"

ALBERT: "AAZARO, EBONY means the dark strength and we kept this name because in that jail there are not mere prisoners but something else."

AAZARO: "What are you trying to say, are they not humans?"

ALBERT: "No, they are evils in the form of humans. In that jail, there are evils that have very unpredictable powers in them. They can't be caught by a single person, but to catch one you need help of many people."

AAZARO: "Why are you telling me this?"

ALBERT: "Because I am feeling the atmosphere around us is changing in such manner that we are not able to predict."

AAZARO: "I promise you ALBERT, I will truly take care of our kingdom."

ALBERT: "Till when, you will take care of this kingdom alone?"

AAZARO: "Alone, how can you say that? You are here, members of the palace are here then how come I am alone."

ALBERT: "I think, you can't make all of us the queen of our kingdom!!"

AAZARO: "ALBERT, what is the hidden meaning behind you click smile?"

ALBERT: "I am saying that the kingdom has got its king but the place of a queen is still vacant."

AAZARO: "I know this, but I don't know whether she will say yes or no."

ALBERT: "Why would she say no to you? She loves you very much and I have seen you both love each other and also can take care of the kingdom in better manner."

AAZARO: "Should I go and propose her?"

ALBERT: "If you think that night is the better time to propose her, than you should go for that." AAZARO understood and went back to the room, while he was leaving the room AEREYNA entered.

AEREYNA: "Did you tell him everything?"

ALBERT: "A little bit is left!!"

AEREYNA: "Or, the whole matter is left?"

ALBERT: "You know this very well, why I didn't tell him the full truth?"

AEREYNA: "AAZARO need to be more careful from now onwards, because I am getting the symbols around me, that something very wrong is going to happen."

ALBERT: "I have warned him!!!"

AEREYNA: "Did you tell him about HALDIS?"

ALBERT: "No, I didn't."

AEREYNA: "Then you should tell him, because you know very well who he is." JUDASE was listening the whole conversation and he went in the room of LAVINZO where LAVINZO was just cutting the leaves of a plant.

JUDASE: "What the hell are you doing, have we come here for this?"

LAVINZO: "sssshhhhhhhhhhhhh!!!!!!! Don't disturb."

JUDASE: "I have got very important information for you."

LAVINZO: "JUDASE didn't your parents tell you anything about manners?"

JUADSE: "Will you please stop doing that!!!!"

LAVINZO: "uuhhhhh!!!! Really you don't know anything about manners. If you would have known about this then you didn't have disturbed me in my work."

JUDASE: "LAVINZO, I am tired of you. I really want to know when you will change."

LAVINZO: "I am not the air who can change the direction at any time but I am just like a shining northern star, which changes the path of others. Just leave this and tell me what information you have got."

JUDASE: "HALDIS!!!!"

LAVINZO: "Where is the stone spirit?"

JUDASE: "He is kept in EBONY."

LAVINZO: "Look outside JUDASE."

JUDASE: "What? I can't see anything new."

LAVINZO: "See the atmosphere is singing the song of love for the lovers and for the people who are prohibited from this."

JUDASE: "Will you please tell me directly!!!!"

LAVINZO: "This is the perfect time for the occasion, ceremony and meetings."

JUADSE: "Meetings!!! What meetings?"

LAVINZO: "Just have the zest of this and let my mind do its work. You know what, from few days my mind has become very lazy, and from your news he will be active just like the previous time. You just enjoy, there are many ceremonies going to be held before the dark appears." The words of LAVINZO indicated towards the vicious future of ANALASKA. He went inside the room of AAZARO and said, "Brother, what are doing there?"

AAZARO: "Nothing, just remembering the days of our childhood."

LAVINZO: "Yes, those were the golden days of my life too."

AAZARO: "I still remember while practicing, you always acted lazy."

LAVINZO: "Yes, and you always used to make excuses to CAPRION for going to jungle in order to find the girl, who scolded you very badly."

AAZARO: "Fine, but I never went to jungle for that sense."

LAVINZO: "What do you think that I don't know that MORENA is that girl? AAZARO looked at him."

AAZARO: "How do you know that?"

LAVINZO: "How do I know that brother!!!!!!? When she is around you, you are just lost in her . . . . you don't even bother about the world then."

AAZARO: "So, for what purpose you have come here?

LAVINZO: "Till when, you and she will be like this? Just stop wasting your time and make her my sister in law as soon as you can."

AAZARO: "What?"

LAVINZO: "What, what do you mean? You don't want to marry her? I mean you love someone else?"

AAZARO: "No, I love her only, but don't you think that it is very soon."

LAVINZO: "Actually, do one thing. Just wait till she get old and you too become the same and then propose her for the marriage, ok?"

AAZARO and LAVINZO they both chuckled and AAZARO said, "by the way, this not a bad idea." After saying this AAZARO began to think on his words, he decided to propose her but in very different manner and LAVINZO left for his room. He did not sleep for the whole night and came to a great conclusion. He got to know, how to propose her for the marriage. That night was the last night for LAVINZO for visiting EBONY. JUDASE didn't have any idea what he was doing, but he had the feeling that something very vicious is going on in his mind. That night LAVINZO entered in the jail EBONY, in order to meet someone. He entered in the jail somehow; he knew where he has to go. He was just looking forward to all the prisoners; they all were quite scary and vicious. They purely looked like an evil but LAVINZO was in search of someone else, someone who is more dangerous. Eventually, he found his target, which was HALDIS. He was looking like a normal man who had simple moustache, long brown hair and black eyes. He appeared to be like handsome personality, but he was under the cob web of heavy chains. LAVINZO just came in front of him and said, "HALDIS how are you?"

HALDIS: "For what purpose you have come here LAVINZO?"

LAVINZO: "Whatever I heard is very less to understand you, my dear stone spirit."

HALDIS: "It's very simple work for an evil to recognize me and my dear; my powers are that what you are calling me but my name is only HALDIS."

LAVINZO: "It's better to be known by your work and I have heard about your deeds too and I know this also, that because of your immense powers you're kept in here."

HALDIS: "Tell me the time and the day when you are taking me out of here? I came to know for what purpose you have come here."

LAVINZO: "I told you, I know you're all the powers. But before we become friends, let's shake hands. Tomorrow is the day." After saying this, LAVINZO began to move back. When HALDIS saw his hands, he saw a map made on his hands which showed the secret path, from where LAVINZO wants him run away from EBONY. HALDIS gave a cunning smile and goes back to his place. Most of the people in the palace were waiting eagerly for the next morning, some for the new life and some for the new line. When LAVINZO came back to his room he found JUDASE standing near his bed.

JUDASE: "I heard about the idea that you have given to AAZARO, your real brother."

LAVINZO: "Do you have rabbit ears?"

JUDASE: "What?"

LAVINZO: "I think, you must be having it that's why you hear everything but understand nothing."

JUDASE: "What do you mean?"

LAVINZO: "I mean that you only take zest of the ceremonies and let me do my work properly. Just trust me JUDASE I will not break your hope." LAVINZO gave a cunning smile to JUDASE and he went to his room.

Most important people of the kingdom were waiting eagerly for tomorrow. Nobody knew that the next morning was going to change the lives of many people. The next beautiful morning was an illusion but in real it was going to be the biggest nightmare for many of the people. There was certain change in atmosphere that was noticed by IRISH at the mid night. He began to talk to himself, "Why this sky is showing such vicious visions to me? it seems to me as if, it is going to open many portals. But what portals, I really don't know about that. But I have understood one thing, tomorrow it's going be the greatest day for the people of ANALASKA." . . . .

"What was the next morning? What was going to happen? Why the shape and color of the sky was quite changed? No one was aware of anything, but everyone was waiting for that beautiful vicious tomorrow."

THE VICIOUS NEW-MOON NIGHT

The next morning MORENA woke up and went to the washroom to get fresh but when she came out of the washroom, she found a dress in royal blue color with some beautiful flowers and a note. She took up the note and read it.

MY LOVELY MORENA,

TODAY I WANT TO SAY SOMETHING TO YOU, BUT AS YOUR AAZARO NOT AS THE LORD. YOU KNOW WE LOVE EACH OTHER BUT TODAY, I WANT TO TALK TO YOU ABOUT SOMETHING VERY IMPORTANT. SO, IN TWILIGHT YOU WILL HAVE TO COME NEAR THE RIVER, MAINLY THAT AREA WHERE WE MEET AT EVERYNIGHT.

YOUR DEAREST AAZARO.

She smiled and decided to not to visit palace today, she began to prepare herself for the evening. That morning LAVINZO was again in the meditation. When JUDASE entered in his room, he saw him meditating. Unfortunately, a very idiotic idea came to his mind; he saw that LAVINZO'S eyes were closed. So, he tried took out his sword. Though, LAVINZO'S eyes were closed but then also he stopped the sword. He turned that sword towards JUADSE and that sword just stopped at the tip of the eyes of JUDASE because LAVINZO stopped that sword by his small sign. LAVINZO laughed and said, "I really hate when someone interrupts me while I am meditating. Don't try to judge me and my powers JUDASE (he opened his eyes). You or anyone in this world can't have any idea about it, let me do my work and you do yours."

JUDASE: "But what I have to do? Except one work, you didn't have given me any task to perform."

LAVINZO: "You already did your job, so you have done your work and now just take the zest."

JUDASE: "Zest, but zest of what?"

LAVINZO: "Zest of my next vicious plan." LAVINZO laughed and went back to his meditation. JUDASE wanted to ask something but when he saw LAVINZO back to his work, he murmured in his self and went out of the room. Everyone was busy in their work but the king was not present in the palace, he was at the place where he has to meet his love in the twilight. He was decorating the area through beautiful flowers of the jungle. He was picking all the flowers of that places where he and MORENA used to spend time, he made bouquets with those flowers and did spread beautiful red golden leaves and many flowers on the floor. When he saw the place became ready for the evening, then he left the place and came back to his palace. He got fresh and took out one beautiful ring from his drawer packed it into a beautiful golden box. He thought that he will make MORENA to wear that ring after she accepts his proposal. On the other hand, in MORENA'S home, LORIYA came to her room and saw the gifts given by AAZARO.

LORIYA: "Oh My god!!!!! I am glad to know that our king has such a great choice. Thank you Miss. MORENA for showing us your gifts and letting us know the great choice of our king."

MORENA: "Will you stop it and please don't behave like that . . . . just help me out to get ready for the evening."

LORIYA: "There is enough time to get ready for the evening."

MORENA: "I know, but can't you see that I am tensed?"

LORIYA (came near to her and held her shoulders): "Don't worry; I will make you look the most beautiful girl of the world."

MORENA: "I know, but I don't know why I am feeling that something wrong is going to happen today. Some bad kind of feelings is coming inside my heart."

LORIYA: "MORENA, will you please stop thinking of bad omens on this good occasion. Just have patience and wait for the evening" MORENA comforted herself with LORIYA'S words and they both began to get ready for tonight. That day something very different was happening with HALDIS. He was noticing his hands again and again in jail, from the afternoon his body began to disappear, but very slowly and gradually . . . . So that none of the soldiers can notify him. From the sunrise AAZARO, MORENA, LAVINZO, JUDASE AND HALDIS were hoping for different things, those things to which they needed badly. "But LAVINZO, what he needed? Means what's going on in his mind? What was his plan? Why did he give AAZARO such suggestion for today only? Why did he want to know about HALDIS? Who is he and what he can do for LAVINZO?" such volume of questions were in the mind of JUDASE.

He was not able to understand him at all. He was thinking that if they both have come here to spread evils and to release evils from EBONY, then "why only HALDIS? Why not all the evils of that jail". He was playing with his own thoughts. The time passed away and the evening came. MORENA got ready and came out of her room.

VAROCIA: "Oh My god!!!!! I never thought my daughter can look so beautiful."

MORENA: "Mother, please stop teasing me."

LORIYA: "Hey, she is not teasing you; you are seriously looking VERY beautiful."

MORENA: "Ok, ok, fine, thank you both of you, now can I leave please?"

VAROCIA: "Off course, my daughter!!!!!" She hugged her mother and came out of her house. She came near to ALMAS and whispered something in his ears and ALMAS moved his head. She got up over him and moved towards her destination. When she reached at the place, she found that area looking extremely beautiful, she found all her favorite flowers and leaves lying down just under her feet, the area was decorated in beautiful manner but something was missing and that was AAZARO, he was not there. Actually, MORENA has reached at that place before time and at that time AAZARO was getting ready in the palace. She was very happy, that night was the new moon night but in the darkness of the sky also, the brightness of love was spreading over the wide range. Suddenly MORENA noticed one of her favorite flower, when she came near to that flower to smell it she noticed its bud with it and when she touched it then unfortunately, a poisonous tiny arrow got stuck near her heart. She saw that in shocked manner and took it out of her body and when she turned back, she saw VOLVO looking her in very angry manner. Slowly and gradually, she was getting unconscious and she fell down. VOLVO came near to her and touched her face in cunning manner and then roared in a werewolf's manner and then holds her hand and went away from there.

While getting ready in the palace, AAZARO heard the voice but neglected it and meditating LAVINZO too heard the voice and then he opened his eyes and gave a cunning smile. While playing with his own thoughts, JUDASE also heard the voice and then he understood the plan of LAVINZO . . . . not fully but something. JUDASE ran towards the room of LAVINZO and he was standing near the balcony.

JUDASE: "I have come to know what your plan was, not fully but some parts of it."

LAVINZO: "You have come across only the incident that took place, but this is a part of the plan . . . . not the whole plan. Just enjoy JUDASE, there are many more things to happen, let's see how much my brother has learnt from his journey." They both smiled cunningly.

AAZARO got ready and took his unicorn RUBIZN and moved towards the river. When he reached their, he thought MORENA will be late today and he began to walk around that place. While walking, something came beneath his shoes; he moved his leg and noticed a very tiny arrow. He picked it up and saw blood.

AAZARO: "This is the blood but of whom? Wait . . . . today only MORENA was about to come here and no one else knew about this place . . . . Except?" AAZARO became extremely angry and he screamed out loud the name of "VOLVOOOOOOOOO".

LAVINZO again heard the voice but this time it was not the voice of a mere king AAZARO but this time it was voice of a real warrior. He again smiled and turns towards JUDASE and said, "Now the adventure begins, let's both of us take zest of this situation." JUDASE again thought that "was this was the plan of LAVINZO to take zest after making someone to go in trouble, is he a fool? Why doesn't he understand that this voice of AAZARO is scaring me a lot, I have never heard such voice from him. Just now he has become so dangerous, even I don't have such courage to go in front of him just now." LAVINZO smiled and said, "This is a part of my plan JUDASE and I am not a fool . . . . I know AAZARO has taken his vicious form and I was waiting for this only and don't worry . . . . nothing is going to happen to you . . . . I will not send you in front of him this time."

JUADSE: "How did you hear my internal voice?"

LAVINZO (kept his hand on JUDASE shoulders): "JUDASE, how many times I have to tell you, I always have ideas about my all friends and enemies. But no one in this world has any idea about my powers." He said such taunting words to him and went outside the room. On the other hand, AAZARO in extremely angry manner began to search VOLVO. He went very deep in the river but couldn't find him.

While he was searching him in the river, he heard some voices and didn't understand anything, he thought that VOLVO is just behind him and took out his sword and turned back. He saw no one, but suddenly he found his legs being tightened by the long leaves. As he saw upwards in his front, a group of giant mosses and plant was there, which spread its leaves and chained him, slowly—slowly these plants were sucking his blood. AAZARO was trying to move himself but his sword fell down and he became helpless. He thought, "this is his last time, he was really hapless for his love, he couldn't be able to save her" While such hopeless thoughts were coming in his mind, he noticed someone coming from upward, he was not visible to him finely but as AAZARO was about to close his eyes that person snatched him from those giant leaves, he took his sword too and they both came out of the river. That person was LEO in his human form.

He helped AAZARO to expel out water from his body. And finally, AAZARO came in consciousness.

LEO: "Don't you know the rules of this river? No one is allowed go in deep, and don't you know this that these giant plants suck the blood of humans, and they kill them because they love to drink the blood of humans."

AAZARO (in cough): "Who are you, how did you save me and why didn't those plants attack on you?"

LEO: "I think you didn't hear me, I said those plant suck the blood of humans."

AAZARO: "Then who are you?" He pointed his sword towards LEO. And suddenly YURA, the mermaid came out of the water.

YURA: "AAZARO, I think you really don't want to stay alive anymore. You have many other ways to kill yourself, please don't try to do this in this sacred river, and if you try it again then this time no one will be able to save you."

AAZARO: "I am in search of someone, someone who came out of this river for the first time, someone who has kidnapped my love."

YURA: "MORENA? What happened to her, where is she?"

AAZARO: "I really don't know where she is, but I know this that VOLVO has kidnapped her, he is the only one who can have the courage to steal my love from me."

YURA: "Look in the sky." All of them looked in the sky and they noticed a thing to which they have never ever seen earlier. The sky was in dark black in color and they saw a river of stars in shinning pink and white color began to flow without any destination, in very fast manner."

LEO: "What is this and where these stars are flowing?" YURA pointed her finger towards the river flow of THALOUS. The THALOUS River which doesn't have any end, which was flowing in continues manner. It rose up in the sky to meet the river of the stars, but the water was on the land and a shiny blue appearance was going to meet somewhere in the sky. It was just felt that THLAOUS is not a mere river but a beautiful woman whose soul is getting released from her body and going to meet her love. Those stars had formed a very bright and beautiful path.

YURA: "You both don't have enough time; I know where he has taken her, LEO you know which form you have to be in. AAZARO, just listen to me very carefully, you think that you can kill him but it's not so easy because he is not a mere evil that can be slaved very easily, you will be needing help and whenever you feel that you want help . . . . Just try to concentrate your mind and call that person to whom you think of that can help you. I bless you and wish you all the best and am aware of the death circle." Apparently, LEO took the shape of a blue lion and very wide and huge white wings came out from his back. AAZARO got shocked and LEO turned towards him.

LEO: "I told you, they love human blood."

AAZARO: "What is happening in the sky? What is a death circle?"

YURA: "This happens only for few hours and after many years this thing has occurred. LEO you have to take AAZARO through this path, to another kingdom where VOLVO has taken MORENA . . . . but be careful!!!! You both have to complete this work very soon, because this path will open the portal for few hours and by will close by itself. If you both didn't find her soon, then you both also will be prisoner there. AAZARO, death circle is like a room which is in the form of circle and just like the coin, it has two phases. Just try to take advantage of that and don't let VOLVO to use his powers . . . . Otherwise no one will be able to save you and her. Hurry you guys don't have enough time."

AAZARO: "But I can only see the meeting of both the rivers, I can't find any portal."

YURA: "You can't see the portal, until and unless you gain such speed that is more than those rivers, you will find more hurdles and LEO will take you out of that. But, listen when you reach near the portal, just cut it in such manner in which it gets open and you will find your destination. Now, don't wait just move fast, you both have very less time remaining with you . . . . So, just go. AAZARO sat on LEO and with the help of the wings, LEO flied towards the sky, he reached at the path and said, "Just hold me very tightly, because I have to gain very high speed". AAZARO held LEO very tightly and they both began to run on the river of stars. Suddenly, they both noticed very massive rocks on their path. Seeing such rocks, LEO generated a pointed horn on his forehead. That horn helped him to diminish those hurdles. He was gaining the speed and they were about to reach at their destination.

AAZARO: "Look there, that's the portal . . . . its good you are gaining the speed, just move ahead." LEO continued with his speed and they both reached at their destination.

LEO: "AAZARO!!!! Be ready you have to make your own way.",

AAZARO: "I am ready." When they reached there at such high speed, LEO didn't stop and AAZARO took his sword, stood up and in sharp manner, cut those rivers vertically. Without any time, they both got entered in the portal and reached at their destination. When they reached, AAZARO saw a very wide and beautiful lake. The whole area was covered with snow but the lake was not freeze and it was quite interesting to note that whole atmosphere was covered with snow, the mountains, the trees except the lake and most shocking thing was that he was not feeling cold at all.

AAZARO: "Where we both have come, why am I not feeling cold and why this lake has not freeze?"

LEO: "Whatever you are seeing is not true but whatever I am seeing is true."

AAZARO: "What do you mean?"

LEO: "AAZARO, this lake name is WARMBURG. But actually this is not any kind of lake; the whole atmosphere that you are noticing is just an illusion . . . . so that none of the mere humans can recognize it."

AAZARO: "Illusion? Then what you are seeing?"

LEO: "This is a volcanic area and this lake is secret path for VOLVO, where he has taken MORENA."

AAZARO: "This means. That you too belong to this kingdom, the evils kingdom." LEO: "Yes, this is true. I belong to this kingdom, but my heart and my emotions don't belong to these people. This is the main reason why I left this kingdom and came to ANALASKA. I wanted to use my powers but not to misuse it."

AAZARO: "Whose kingdom is this? Tell me the name of that person!!!"

LEO: "Though, I left this kingdom but I have never been dishonest with this kingdom. I don't want myself to be called as a traitor, kindly pardon me but I can't tell you the name of that king."

AAZARO: "As you wish, but let me tell you one thing that I will find this out by myself. Now, just tell that how I can reach near to her?"

LEO: "You have to go inside this lake."

AAZARO: "Inside this lake!!!!! But how?"

LEO: "I told you!!!!! Everything you are seeing here is an illusion. You will enter in this, but this area is fully dark. Only the eyes of a werewolf can see in it. And, AAZARO always remember that an evil doesn't like to see its own face."

AAZARO: "If there is only darkness, then how will I find my way?" LEO closed his eyes by his hands and said, "AAZARO, you are a warrior but this time your anger has covered your mind. How can you forget your task of the quest? How can you forget everything that you learned from your journey? You just have to use the third lesson of your quest. You only have to concentrate on my voice, I am well acquainted with the paths of this kingdom and I will tell you your way. Don't forget the words of YURA." AAZARO was in very aggressive mood and his golden nerve which was been disappearing since quite some time, got revived.

AAZARO with his closed eyes turned towards the lake and began to walk according to the instructions given by the LEO. AAZARO entered in the lake, it was full of darkness, and LEO was telling him the ways.

LEO: "AAZARO, just walk straight, you will find two big tunnels just wait and let me think where he might have taken MORENA." AAZARO'S eyes were closed but he just went near to the paths and came towards the first path and touched the floor and then he touched the floor of another tunnel and said, "MORENA is taken from this path."

LEO: "how can you say that?"

AAZARO: "The first whole path had the foot prints of VOLVO, but the essence of her is not here and the second path has her essence, I know VOLVO has made the first path for me because he knew that I will only follow his footprints.",

LEO: "Great!!! Just move ahead."

When he entered in the second tunnel that was a very big area to which AAZARO was not able to see but LEO was able to see it. He found MORENA and told AAZARO.

LEO: "AAZARO, just move left to your path and simply take small steps." AAZARO was taking small steps and he came near to the cob of a spider.

LEO: "AAZARO, MORENA is chained in this cob of spider.", While he was releasing her out, he heard the voice of someone from his back.

That was the voice of VOLVO. He attacked on him from the back and AAZARO fell on the floor.

VOLVO: "You are so late; I thought you will be coming early."

AAZARO: "I am always on time, I expected this only from you're backstab." They both began to fight and VOLVO was getting dominant over AAZARO. VOLVO made AAZARO to fall down and showed that a big spider was getting closer to MORENA. He was becoming hopeless and at then only LEO spoke to him.

LEO: "AAZARO, find out the path of death circle, just find it out." AAZARO just began to look here and there and suddenly VOLVO attacked on him again, he pulled him and threw him on the floor. When AAZARO fell down, he noticed that this sand is not the floor but it's like a bog and it needs more weight. AAZARO ran towards MORENA and cut the chain of her from one side of her hand and gave her a small and useful knife. VOLVO looked this and began to attack on AAZARO. Somehow AAZARO made him to come near to him in order to take him at that place. VOLVO jumped on AAZARO and the sand slipped up and then they both fell down. They both fell in a room that was circular in form. AAZARO understood what YURA was trying to tell him, he was wounded very badly but then also he had to fight. Again the fight began and again VOLVO was getting dominant over AAZARO and this time AAZARO fell on floor in soulless manner. On the other hand, MORENA came in conscious mode . . . . she found a knife in her hand and also saw a giant spider coming towards her, she just inserted that knife in the mouth of that spider and began to release her other hand from the chain of the web. When VOLVO saw AAZARO being soulless, he just began to walk out of the room. AAZARO being soulless closed his eyes and called for help and he called YURA to help him. Having connection with AAZARO, the thing was felt by YURA and she said something that AAZARO had to follow. When AAZARO saw VOLVO going back, he took up his sword and stood up. He pointed his sword on the wall of the room and began to run in circular manner and he hit VOLVO and he fell down. When he completed the circle, he stopped and took out his sword. VOLVO also got up and roared, he ran towards AAZARO in order to hit him but AAZARO ran from that place and VOLVO hit the wall by chance, and in angry manner turned towards AAZARO again. But something happened that was noticed by both of them. Water began to come out of the wall from the cracks and the wall made up of the sand began to shine. When VOLVO saw towards the wall he became scared, he just started shouting and fell down on the floor, he began to hide out his own face. AAZARO just chuckled and said, "An evil is always afraid of his own face". AAZARO picked up his sword and attacked on VOLVO. This time VOLVO was only shouting and was not at all able to attack AAZARO and just like YURA said, AAZARO took the advantage of the room and finally attacked on his head through his sword.

He inserted sword in the middle of the head where the powers of werewolf is concentrated. This time VOLVO lost his powers and his strength too and he fell down on the floor. AAZARO with his sword moved towards the wall and the water, which was coming out turned into a ladder for him and AAZARO came up. He found MORENA being on the floor. He took her in his arms.

AAZARO: "MORENA, MORENA, are you fine?"

MORENA (holding his hand): "I am fine!!!" They both got up and came out of the cave where LEO was standing.

MORENA: "LEO, you helped him, thank you!!!!"

LEO: "It was just my duty, or can say a best friend's responsibility. AAZARO let's go, we need to hurry, the portal is about to get closed." AAZARO and MORENA sat on LEO, they flew and they heard the voice werewolf again. When they turned back, they saw many werewolves roaring and they also began to fly and followed LEO.

AAZARO: "This is the only thing you were not telling me, that this is the kingdom werewolves and VOLVO is the king of this kingdom.",

LEO: "VOLVO is not the king and we need to reach fast." The portal was getting smaller and when they were about to cross, a werewolf attacked on the wings of LEO and LEO just got misbalanced. AAZARO with his sword killed that werewolf and they crossed the portal and the portal got closed." The werewolves were not able to follow them, at all. They came back to their kingdom safely. They landed at that place where AAZARO was about to propose MORENA. They both got off from LEO.

AAZARO: "I am so thankful to you, because of you only I am able to get MORENA back."

LEO: "I just said, you can call it as friend's responsibility." MORENA touched his wings and said, "Not just only a friend but a best friend." She hugged him and said, "Now don't you dare to say that you have to go."

LEO: "I have to go, but I will come back whenever and wherever you need me. I just wish, you both stay together always. My best wishes are with you." After saying these words he went back in the THALOUS River which again began to flow. MORENA had tears in her eyes and AAZARO turned her towards him.

AAZARO: "I told you, when I am with you, you will be safe, and I want you to make safe forever." He moved towards the land, near the flowers he picked up a shell kept on the leaf. He opened it and took out the ring from inside of it. He came near to her and bends down on his knees and said, "MISS MORENA, will you marry me?"

MORENA gave her finger to him and he made her to wear that ring and then took her in his arms and then, they kissed each other. They went back to their homes. AAZARO came to MORENA'S house and they both saw CAPRION and VAROCIA waiting for them.

VAROCIA: "Where were you MORENA? I was scared!!" AAZARO came near to VAROCIA and CAPRION AND said, "SIR CAPRION and MADAM VAROCIA I want to marry your daughter." CAPRION and VAROCIA stood up.

CAPRION: "But, AAZARO you are the king and we don't belong to your level."

AAZARO: "You both are humans, and you both belong to mankind . . . . That's enough for me. I promise I will always keep your daughter happy; I will always take care of her. Just trust me." CAPRION came near to him and hugged him.

CAPRION: "We trust you my lord." All of them became happy and then AAZARO moved for his palace. In the palace, LAVINZO came in the room of JUDASE.

LAVINZO: "Pack the bags and get ready to move towards our kingdom."

JUDASE: "You lost!!! AAZARO won!!!"

LAVINZO: "Did I hear the right thing that I lost?"

JUDASE: "Yes, you heard right. You lost and AAZARO won. He got MORENA from VOLVO, and your trust worthy VOLVO is dead." LAVINZO turned towards JUDASE and said, "When did I say that MORENA is part of my plan and when did say that I trust VOLVO and when did I say that he is dead?"

JUDASE: "If she was not the part of your plan, then why did you include her?"

LAVINZO: "I included her, because I wanted to see that my blood can chase me or not, but I am afraid to tell you that he is not at all able to defeat me. And as far as VOLVO'S matter is concerned, I think he needs some time to relax because now we don't need him at all. Let him relax in the DEATH CIRCLE."

JUDASE: "Relax? Are you mad, he is dead?"

LAVINZO: "JUDASE, I told you to get ready and to get back to the kingdom. Our work is finished over here."

JUDASE: "NO!!! LAVINZO, this time I want to know everything which is going under your head, tell me now.

LAVINZO: "YURA only told the half part about the DEATH CIRCLE, but she forgot another face of the coin."

JUADSE: "What do you mean?"

LAVINZO: "YURA only told how he will be killed, but she forgot that advantage of the circle can only be taken once, not every time."

JUADSE: "You mean, VOLVO is still alive?"

LAVINZO: "I didn't say this, but I said let him take rest now."

JUDASE: "Is that AAZARO has committed any mistake?"

LAVINZO: "He has committed the biggest mistake of his life, his warrior hand has now turned to a mere human that is the only thing that I wanted to do. He has trusted a traitor who belongs to my kingdom."

JUDASE: "Who is it?"

LAVINZO: "I told you we have enough time. Now will you please prepare to move?"

JUDASE: "And, what about HALDIS?"

LAVINZO: "I have done his arrangements too." They both gave a cunning smile to each other.

When AAZARO returned to the palace, he saw LAVINZO going back to his kingdom. AAZARO came near to him and said, "Brother where you are going?"

LAVINZO: "Just going to back to my kingdom."

AAZARO: "This is yours kingdom too."

LAVINZO: "I know brother, but I have got some urgent work related to my kingdom. I have to go, but I promise I will be back very soon."

AAZARO: "When the golden days are going to come back?"

LAVINZO: "Very soon!!!! Can say only after few days, when you will be marrying your love." They both hugged and LAVINZO left. AAZARO went back to the palace. He became fresh and went to sleep. But the night did not end there. During early in the morning, LEO came from balcony to the room of AAZARO and took his human form. He took out a sword from his back and went near to AAZARO. It was the sword of AAZARO. He kept at its place and the sword that AAZARO was using got disappeared. He quietly came out of the room and took his lion form and went away.

On the other hand, HALDIS became invisible and he came out of the prison. He was running very fast and he went in the jungle where he found the hut of his beloved EDANA. He went in that hut.

HALDIS: "EDANA, EDANA!!!! See your love HALDIS has come." EDANA came out of the room. She ran towards him and kissed him.

EDANA: "HALDIS how are you or you fine and did lord allow you to go, how you came here?" HALDIS hugged her very tightly and said, "You know it very well, that I can't be allowed to go because of the powers I have." She left him and said, "Did you escape from there? Is it that you are going to use your powers again?"

HALDIS: "Yes, I escaped from there but this time . . . . I promise I will not misuse my powers."

EDANA: "Why you have escaped from there, and who helped you?"

HALDIS: "LAVINZO helped me and he wants to take me to his kingdom, but before proceeding there I wanted to meet you."

EDANA: "He will use you and your powers too. Don't go there, just surrender."

HALDIS: "I promise, I will not misuse my powers but also I don't want to go back to prison. I want to start my new life with you; I don't want myself to be far from you. LAVINZO has given me the chance to live my new life with you. So, just don't disappoint me please, I beg you, I really can't live without you anymore." EDANA again kissed him and said, "Even I want to live my life with you, but how is it possible?"

HALDIS: "We will be safe in LAVINZO'S kingdom but you have to wait for some time. For now, I have to hide myself anywhere and after some days I will go to his kingdom."

EDANA: "I agree!!! But remember my words HALDIS, I will be with you till you are good and if you did something that is unpredictable . . . . for then mind it on that day, EDANA is out of your life."

HALDIS: "I made a promise, I made a commitment and I love you!!!! No one else is there in my life except you. And, I can never break my promise to you." They both got very close, looked into each other's eyes and they kissed each other.

That night for the first time HALDIS and EDANA got intimated and they became closer than earlier. The night got over and the morning sun came out of the vicious clouds with a bright smile. The whole

ANALASKA got up from a very deep night. Before AAZARO woke up, ALBERT CRUZ came to his room.

ALBERT: "AAZARO, wake up!!!" AAZARO got up from his dreams.

AAZARO: "OH!!! NO!!!"

ALBERT: "What happened?"

AAZARO: "ALBERT, in the morning the first face that I saw, is of yours. Shit!!!!"

ALBERT: "Why, what so dangerous is about my face?"

AAZARO: "There is nothing dangerous about your face, but the news that you will tell me after my ablution." ALBERT laughed and said, "a king must not take rest this much. So, get ready for the assembly."

AAZARO: "Now, will you please give me some time to get ready?"

ALBERT: "OK, my lord."

AAZARO got ready and every important member of the palace and the TYMONE'S court too assembled in the hall.

AN IMMORTAL CURSE

ALL the people were waiting for AAZARO to come. As he came, he sat on throne.

ALBERT CRUZ: "I want to make a special announcement that our king AAZARO has found someone who is perfect for that position that is the queen's position of ANALASKA. And it's none other than MISS MORENA, who is choice of our king." MORENA stood up; ALBERT held her hands and took her near to AAZARO. AAZARO also stood up from the throne and ALBERT gave her hand in the hands of AAZARO.

ALBERT: "In coming few days, there will be the huge celebration of their wedding and all of you and the whole ANALASKA is invited." Everyone stood from their places and a huge sound of clapping came. MORENA and AAZARO looking in each other's eyes, very happily; they were very happy after many days. But very dangerous news came to the ears of ALBERT. When the assembly got over then ALBERT called ALEC, AAZARO, MORENA and VIRONCCE. They all assembled in the hall.

AAZARO: "Why you have called us?"

ALBERT: "There is very big news!!!"

MORENA: "About whom?"

ALBERT: "About a prisoner who has escaped from EBONY."

AAZARO: "You mean an evil?"

ALBERT: "Yes, an evil!!!!"

VIRONCCE: "who is he?"

ALBERT: "I have got this information from soldiers that HALDIS has escaped from the prison and no one knows how."

AAZARO: "How this can happen? How he can escape? No one saw him? Where the hell were the soldiers?"

ALBERT: "I don't think that he has escaped by his own but I feel that someone has helped him to do so because the security over there is very high."

MORENA: "We all should not forget that he has vicious powers which he can use on anyone, we all need to be alert regarding this matter."

ALBERT: "VIRONCCE, you can feel his warmth. So, just use your powers and let us know that where is he?"

VIRONCCE: "I can only tell you whether he is in this kingdom or not, and if he would have left this kingdom then I can't tell where he has gone." VIRONCCE closed his eyes for few seconds and said, "He is still here, in this kingdom, ask all the soldiers to go to the jungle area, I think he is there only." AAZARO ordered his few army men to search HALDIS near the jungle area. After this everyone went on their work but MORENA went to the jungle to meet his very good friend IRISH. She, along with ALMAS went to the hut of IRISH. When she reached, she found IRISH was picking some mangoes from the tree. He was standing on the ladder. Seeing MORENA he became glad and said, "OH! I am the last person to whom you have come to invite?"

MORENA: "IRISH, how do you know that I came and how you know about my marriage?" IRISH came on the land and smiled while looking on MORENA.

IRISH: "I guess there is not any kind of secret or news regarding my kingdom which is unknown to me."

MORENA: "So, I am here to invite you for my wedding. Will you come?"

IRISH: "I don't know my dear."

MORENA: "Why not?"

IRISH: "Just tell me one thing that your vicious dream that scares you has stopped?"

MORENA: "Yes, off course!!! I wanted to tell you that those dreams have got their end and look at my nerves they have turned to human nerves. I think the curse that I had has ended now." IRISH held her hands and looked on it in sorrowful manner.

MORENA: "IRISH, what happened? Don't you think that all these things happened to just make me and my love to get rid of this curse? I am very happy now, I can't tell but I can't find you being happy."

IRISH: "When our nightmares stops by themselves, then always remember that they have found another way to scare you."

MORENA: "What do you mean IRISH?"

IRISH: "Just tell me one thing, how much you love AAZARO?"

MORENA: "More than my life!!!!"

IRISH: "And, what you can do for him in order to save him?"

MORENA: "Anything!!!! I can take anyone's life and even I can give my life too.",

IRISH: "_WHEN DESTINY DEFINES YOUR LOVE AN IMMORTAL CURSE OF YOUR LIFE THEN WHAT YOU WILL CHOOSE, LIVE_

*YOUR LIFE WITHOUT YOUR LOVE OR LEAVE YOUR LIFE FOR
YOUR LOVE?",*

MORENA: "Today, will you please tell me that what is the curse on
me and on my love?"

IRISH: "I am sorry, I can't because one day by yourself you will get
to know what curse you have and always remember, just now you are
a girl but after few days you will be the queen of the kingdom and
then a time will come in your life when you will have to make many
important decisions then at that time don't be a lover but being a
responsible queen, try to make the correct decisions which will not be
beneficial to you only but to everyone in the kingdom and mind my
words don't make mistake like JUBEELIA. Now, just go, it's late now."

MORENA: "I don't know what will happen tomorrow and what you
are still hiding from me, but I just want to tell you that I will be waiting
on my wedding day for one of my best friend who saved my life."

IRISH: MORENA, i want to alert you for one thing.

MORENA: What is that IRISH?

IRISH: hardly matters that yours and AAZARO'S nerves have turned
to normal humans but be careful, never let anyone to hurt that hand
of AAZARO.

MORENA: why, so?

IRISH: because till now we all have seen only one face of the coin the
another face is still hidden and if anyone did something to that hand
then even god will not be able to the doom.

MORENA: i really, don't have any idea what you are talking about
but i will surely be careful about it.

After saying these words MORENA and ALMAS left. While she
was leaving, IRISH eyes got filled with tears and he said, "If I were a

destiny maker, then I would have changed your destiny, which is not going to show any mercy on you or on your love. My best wishes are with you but it's useless to say because someone will make not only hurdles but will create disasters in your life. I really don't have any idea, that till when you will be able to tolerate." On the other hand, HALDIS was leaving the kingdom from the path of the jungle. Luck by chance MORENA encountered HALDIS.

MORENA: "Who are you?"

HALDIS: "I am a shepherd, coming from BRIZON'S kingdom."

MORENA: "For what purpose?"

HALDIS: "Well, I have heard many things about ANALASKA'S beauty. So, just wanted to see it."

MORENA: "Oh! So, you are a visitor?"

HALDIS: "Yes, and you MISS?"

MORENA: "I am MORENA, daughter of CAPRION. And, you?"

HALDIS: "My name is HAL . . . . UH AVON, AVON."

MORENA: "OH! Nice to meet you AVON, do you want any help?"

HALDIS: "No, not at all, I am fine."

MORENA: "Should I drop you? Because this area is not very much safe."

HALDIS: "No, I am fine and after sometime I will move towards the kingdom by myself, thanks for asking."

MORENA: "Ok, nice to meet you. Bye!!!!"

HALDIS: "Bye!!!"

HALDIS moved from there but by mistake he dropped his band, which he used to wear and MORENA saw it. She shouted for him but he went away and she also came back to the palace. When she came, she ran to meet ALBERT. ALBERT saw the band in her hand.

ALBERT: "MORENA, what is it? Show me."

MORENA: "Oh! This band!!! Actually I encountered a person in the jungle who came from BRIZON'S kingdom, he was a visitor."

ALBERT: "Are you sure he was a visitor?"

MORENA: "Why are you asking me like this?"

ALBERT: "Look at the band carefully; it's a band to which every prisoner of the EBONY wears."

MORENA: "Means, he was?"

ALBERT: "Yes, he was HALDIS." MORENA began to move back but this time ALBERT stopped her.

ALBERT: "Where did you encounter him?"

MORENA: "Just now, in the jungle."

ALBERT: "It means, by now he would have left our kingdom."

MORENA: "What do you mean ALBERT; we should only sit like that?"

ALBERT: "NO, my dear one. But I am saying, that now no one will be able to find him."

MORENA: "So, we should sit like that and wait for his attack?"

ALBERT: "I think you didn't hear me, I said he must have left our kingdom."

MORENA: "Then what we should do?"

ALBERT: nothing my dear, there is anything to find out. I know why he has escaped?"

MORENA: "Why?"

ALBERT: "He also loves someone as AAZARO loves you, I think for her he has escaped and I also think that this time he will not miss use his powers."

MORENA: "How you can be so sure?"

ALBERT: "Because, the girl to whom he loves is just like you and she had consoled him to stay away from bad things."

MORENA: "How do you know this?"

ALBERT: "Because I know about that girl EDANA, last night she came to me and told me everything and before this also . . . . She told me about him when he was misusing his powers."

MORENA: "Did she tell you anything, that where he is going now and if there was something like that, and then why didn't you tell AAZARO about it and what you were doing in the hall. And, is it she a trust worthy person?"

ALBERT: "She is not only trust worthy but a patriot too, and this matter was between me and her only, no one else is involved. So, it would be better to let him start his new life, don't interrupt."

MORENA: "Fine, but if he comes back and misused his powers then?"

ALBERT: "Then, she will again come to me to tell about his deeds."

MORENA: "Ok!!!! ALBERT, I trust on your words but I don't trust her."

ALBERT: "I promise, I will not disappoint you our new queen. "They both smiled and MORENA went to the room of AAZARO. He was standing in the balcony, from where he always used to see his kingdom. She went close to him and closed his eyes from the back.

AAZARO: "Is it the queen or my any other girlfriend?"

MORENA left him and said from the back, "who is your other girlfriend?" AAZARO held her hand pulled her in his front and said, "MORENA, she is my everything, even more than my life." MORENA felt shy and said, "I went in the jungle to invite IRISH."

AAZARO: "Really, what he said?"

MORENA: "He wasn't looking sure and he told me something that was scary." AAZARO held her face and said, "as I told you, when I am with you . . . . no one can hurt you, I will be shield and I will love you forever."

MORENA: "Till when?"

AAZARO: "Till my last breath!!!!"

MORENA: "Promise?"

AAZARO: "Promise!!! Not only now, but whenever you will need me I will surly come in every birth and we will stay like this forever, forever and forever." It was the pink evening again, when they were talking and looking in each other's eyes and they kissed each other while holding each other very tightly. They off course forgot that the happiness is always followed by the tears.

On the other hand, LAVINZO'S mind plans were getting successful. While LAVINZO was making some plans in his room JUDASE as usual broke the silence.

JUDASE: "What the hell you are doing now?"

LAVINZO: "I am playing cards, would you like to join?"

JUDASE: "I AM NOT JOKING."

LAVINZO: "Am I joking? No, not at all, my dear one!!!"

JUDASE: "What do you think, what are you doing now?"

LAVINZO: "I am preparing my army for the war, but one thing is missing!!!" HALDIS came from the door and said, "The missing person of your army has come." JUDASE became quite shocked.

LAVINZO: "Welcome, the stone spirit. Now it's perfect time to prepare the army for the war."

JUDASE: "But this time is the celebration time for ANALASKAN'S."

LAVINZO: "Yes, off course, the last celebration!!!!"

JUDASE: "What do you mean?"

LAVINZO: "I mean, my lovely brother and his beloved think that this is the end of their curse but . . . . it's the beginning of their curse and IRISH was right when nightmares stops then we need to be scared more because they finds some other way to follow and I am their biggest nightmare.",

HALDIS: "So, what is your plan?"

LAVINZO: "HALDIS, I thought you are like me but its ok. Just be ready and prepare our army, because very soon I have to make my brother realize his curse." They all laughed in evil form . . . .

"What was going to happen? What was LAVINZO'S plan? No one was aware about it. But, as whatever written in the destiny no one knows like that only what was going in the mind of LAVINZO no one thought. But apart from this, AAZARO and MORENA were preparing for their wedding and LAVINZO was preparing for the biggest surprising gift of their wedding."

THE TRUTH MIRROR

As everyone was preparing for the wedding, each and every person of the palace as well as of the kingdom was engaged with the different work. A wave of happiness had pierced everyone's heart but a person was missing who was about to play an important role in the lives of MORENA and AAZARO. "Who was that?" ALBERT CRUZ went to his home. He found AEREYNA talking to the made.

ALBERT: "Where is our son?"

AEREYNA: "Where he can be? In his room!!!" ALBERT with click smile went to his room. When he entered in the room he found many mirrors, very beautiful mirrors of different designs. He saw LUCAS working on the design of a new, but very big mirror.

ALBERT: "Till when you will be engaged in the work?"

LUCAS: "I can ask the same question."

ALBERT: "You must have heard about the royal wedding."

LUCAS: "About AAZARO and MORENA, for them only I am working so hard." ALBERT came near to him; he was seeing his son after so many days or can say months. LUCAS had grown up, having very French style beard and moustache. He was not looking on his father because they were not at all close to each other.

ALBERT: "So, this is the gift for them?"

LUCAS: "No, but it's the biggest gift. She is waiting for it eagerly."

ALBERT: "Are you serious? She hasn't even seen you!!!"

LUCAS: "When did I say that she has seen me? I just said that she is waiting for the gift eagerly?"

ALBERT: "How do you know this? And what do you mean that it is for MORENA?"

LUCAS: "Father, these are not mere mirrors, it tells the truth and MORENA will need it very soon!!!!"